"I don't remember ever being held, being kissed." Tears welled in her eyes. "How can I not remember anything?"

"I don't know." The thought that he'd been the first man in her memory to touch her lips with his was so erotic and at the same time so humbling.

He touched her shoulder and she stepped into his arms again. He nuzzled her silky, sweet-smelling hair. "The theory of amnesia is that you're blocking out memories that are too painful or too awful to deal with. It's called dissociative amnesia. It's generally caused by a traumatic event."

Her hand went to her temple. He wasn't sure if she was touching the scar or massaging a headache.

"I promise you. I'm going to find out who did this to you and I'm going to make sure he pays."

MALLORY KANE

DEATH OF A BEAUTY QUEEN

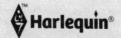

TORONTO NEW YORK LONDON
AMSTERDAM PARIS SYDNEY HAMBURG
STOCKHOLM ATHENS TOKYO MILAN MADRID
PRAGUE WARSAW BUDAPEST AUCKLAND

I dedicate this book to the people of New Orleans: their hearts, their courage, their indestructible optimism.
Laissez les bon temps rouler!

Recycling programs
for this product may
not exist in your area.

ISBN-13: 978-0-373-74677-4

DEATH OF A BEAUTY QUEEN

ABOUT THE AUTHOR

Mallory has two very good reasons for loving reading and writing. Her mother was a librarian, who taught her to love and respect books as a precious resource. Her father could hold listeners spellbound for hours with his stories. He was always her biggest fan.

She loves romantic suspense with dangerous heroes and dauntless heroines, and enjoys tossing in a bit of her medical knowledge for an extra dose of intrigue. After twenty-five books published, Mallory is still amazed and thrilled that she actually gets to make up stories for a living.

Mallory lives in Tennessee with her computer-genius husband and three exceptionally intelligent cats. She enjoys hearing from readers. You can write her at mallory@mallorykane.com or via Harlequin Books.

Books by Mallory Kane

*Ultimate Agents
**Black Hills Brotherhood
‡‡The Delancey Dynasty

CAST OF CHARACTERS

Dixon Lloyd—This NOPD detective failed to solve the Beauty Queen Murders twelve years ago. Now he has a second chance. But he has led the killer to Rose. This time he *will* save her, even if it breaks his guarded heart.

Rosemary Delancey/Rose Bohéme—Attacked and left for dead, she remembers nothing before waking up in the care of a motherly Cajun woman. Now her past has caught up with her. Her safety and her heart lie in the hands of the sexy, determined detective who never gave up on finding her.

Aron Wasabe—An accomplished hit man, Wasabe is haunted by his first victim, who disappeared before he could finish her off. Now he has a second chance to kill her and get out from under the thumb of the man who ordered her death, the Boss.

The Boss—He's waited years for revenge. Once Rosemary is dead, the last link tying him to the Beauty Queen Murders will be broken, and her inherited fortune will be his.

Lyndon Banker—Rosemary's fiancé, spoiled and in debt to loan sharks, was murdered that night. The police wondered if the killer was really after the wealthy compulsive gambler and Rosemary was merely collateral damage.

Sheldon Banker—This wealthy businessman disowned his son because of his gambling debts. Does that make him responsible for Lyndon's and Rosemary's deaths?

Junior Fulbright—The city councilman's son is in deep with the Beauty Queen killer. But does he know who's really running the show?

Councilman Fulbright—The influential, ambitious city councilman is so hard on crime, he let his own son go to prison. What else will he do to stop crime in New Orleans?

Prologue

Twelve Years Ago

It was an ugly crime scene. Not that newly appointed Detective Dixon Lloyd had seen many—none as a detective, but this one was worse than most. He could tell by the other officers' faces.

Blood was smeared on walls, on floors, on the snow-white sheets on the young woman's bed. A terry cloth robe's sash had been cut in two and tied to the two headboard posts. Dixon grimaced as his stomach churned.

He stepped into the bathroom, which didn't help his queasiness. Water filled the large spa tub about two-thirds full. A glass of white wine sat on the imported Italian tile surrounding the tub and a pale ivory candle had burned down to the wick.

The room appeared ready for the beauty to sweep in, slide an elegant dressing gown off her shoulders and sink into the warm, pleasantly scented water.

Only the water wasn't warm or pleasantly scented. It was cold. And red. Bloodred.

Dixon's gaze zeroed in on the smeared handprint on the tile near the glass. She must have reached for it, hoping to break it and use it as a weapon. But the smear stopped two inches from the base of the glass. She hadn't been quick enough. He swallowed acrid saliva as a vision of what must have happened rose in his brain. He tried to concentrate on searching for anything unusual about the scene, other than the obvious.

"—make of it?" It was the voice of his partner and mentor, veteran detective James Shively, talking to the crime scene investigators in the bedroom.

"Hard to say," the CSI replied. "There's blood smeared everywhere, but the only spatter is on the bed. I'd guess he used a slender blade."

"Yeah," Shively said. "How much blood are we talking about?"

"With the blood in the bathwater and who knows how much down the drain, not to mention all this rain going down the sewer drains, too, it's going to be hard to tell."

Dix looked back at the tub. Down the drain. The killer must have surprised her in the bedroom, tied her to the bed and tortured her, then thrown her in the tub so that her lifeblood dripped down the drain.

"Say, Shively," the CSI went on, "the name on the apartment is Rosemary Delancey. Wasn't she Queen of Carnival this past Mardi Gras?"

"Yeah, not to mention the oldest granddaughter of Con Delancey."

"Oh hell," the CSI breathed as Dixon joined them. Dixon had heard of the Delanceys. Of course—who hadn't? Everyone around here knew who they were. Con Delancey, the late, infamous senator from Louisiana, was as famous as Huey Long and his brother in this part of the country. And as scandalous.

Con Delancey's granddaughter had been murdered. Which meant that this story would headline local and national news tomorrow and who knew how many more days. And the department would be under the gun to catch the killer. He raised his gaze to Shively's.

"Yeah," Shively said and nodded, reading his mind. "Welcome to Homicide, Lloyd. You're in luck. Your first homicide investigation is going to be the most sensational murder New Orleans has seen in a long time."

Dixon glanced at the bed. On the floor beside the bedside table was a small gold photo frame. It lay facedown and he could see shards of glass surrounding it. He picked it up and turned it over. The girl in the picture had on a gaudy tiara and was dressed in a silver evening gown. Over her head was a banner that read "Queen of Carnival."

His gaze slid over the smeared and stained sheets. One particular stain looked like it had been made by the bloody side of a face—the same beautiful face as in the picture—pressed against the material. He swallowed again, not quite free of the nauseating vision of how she must have struggled. How she must have screamed and fought and even pleaded with her attacker not to kill her.

He took the back off the picture frame and slid the photo out, shaking the bits of glass off it.

"Be nice if we had a body," he said.

Chapter One

Present Day

Aron Wasabe groped in the dark for his cell phone on the bedside table and turned off the ringer before it could buzz again. He squinted at the display and grimaced, then threw back the covers and got up, sliding the phone into the pocket of his pajamas.

His wife, Carol, turned over. "Aron?" she whispered. "Don't forget Amy's soccer game. It's at six."

He leaned over and kissed her forehead. "Go back to sleep," he muttered. She sighed softly. She was used to the phone calls and odd work hours. After all these years, she didn't even ask questions.

Down in the kitchen, he started a pot of coffee, then gazed out the patio doors at the rising sun while it perked.

The president of Aron Accounting, Bruce Wexler, had worked for him for years. He was smart and capable. There wasn't much he couldn't handle. So if he thought something was important enough to call Wasabe this early, it probably was. It might even be important enough to warrant his having to work on Friday. He frowned. It had better not take too long. He was not going to miss another one of his daughter's soccer games.

He decided to finish his first cup of coffee before calling Wexler back.

After filling a mug, he added a generous dollop of cream and three heaping spoonfuls of sugar. Then he walked out onto the patio where the sun bathed the flowers and trees in pale pink light.

He smiled to himself. Carol would probably call it mauve or puce or some other ridiculous word. She did a good job with the house and the yard. The patio was like an outdoor kitchen and dining room, beautifully landscaped.

She'd made a home for him and their six-year-old daughter and he loved her for it. He sat down in a glider and gently rocked back and forth as he enjoyed that first swallow of coffee of the day. It was the best.

His phone rang again. He took another long swallow before leisurely retrieving it. He checked the display. Wexler again.

"Bruce? Twice before seven? This better be good." Wasabe allowed a slight irritation to color his voice, just enough to worry the president of his accounting firm.

"It's important, Mr. Wasabe. There's a kid running his mouth. Says he saw the Delancey girl. The one who was murdered twelve years ago. The Carnival Queen?"

Wasabe's throat closed on a sip of coffee. He coughed. "So?" he asked, clearing his throat and trying to sound casual, but hearing the anxiety in his voice. "That's what you woke me up for? Some yahoo trying to sell a bill of goods, like we hear every week?"

It couldn't be true. Rosemary Delancey couldn't be alive. Not after all this time. But a flutter of hope tickled the back of his throat. If she were…

"I know how you like Delancey stuff," Wexler went on. "So I knew you'd want to hear about this."

Wasabe had given his employees and associates hints over the years of his interest in the Delancey family. He'd never explained why. He'd left it to them to draw their own conclusions. Apparently, the majority of them believed he was obsessed with the infamous late-patriarch of the clan, Con Delancey.

Wexler was still talking and he'd missed most of it. "What did you say?" he asked.

"I said the kid is James Fulbright's boy."

"The loudmouth? He's Councilman Fulbright's son?"

"Yeah. He's saying his pop was King of Krewe *Ti Malice* the year the Delancey girl was Carnival Queen."

"Was he?" Wasabe asked. Wexler should know. The Wexlers had ridden in Mardi Gras parades for decades.

"Yes, sir. He sure was. Junior was probably about twelve. He claims she was his first crush. Said he'd recognize her in a whorehouse under a sweaty fat john."

"How'd you hear about this?"

"Junior was bragging. He told me T-Bo Pereau was hanging around. Said Pereau sneaked off like a pup that had just snatched a bone away from a big dog."

"And who the hell is T-Bo Pereau?"

"A nobody. In and out of prison for possession and small-time dealing."

"Keep an eye on Pereau, and bring Junior Fulbright to the office. Noon. He knows Rosemary so well, he can find her for us. And if he talks to anybody else I'll cut off his thumbs." Wasabe grimaced. "And don't be late. I'm going to my daughter's soccer game at six."

"Yes, sir."

Wasabe hung up and picked up his coffee with a shaky hand. Twelve years ago, while working a small-time collector for a loan shark, he'd made a choice that earned him a lucrative career as a contract killer. However, it left him effectively indentured to a powerful and ruthless man.

Was this his chance to close the book on that first botched job? If Rosemary Delancey really was alive, maybe he could finally earn his freedom by delivering her to The Boss.

IT WAS HER. He was sure of it. Detective Dixon Lloyd's pulse hammered in his ears. That two-bit drug dealer he and his partner, Ethan Delancey, had collared for parole violation was right, and Ethan was wrong.

T-Bo Pereau had sworn he could tell them where Rosemary Delancey, the supposedly murdered Carnival Queen, was, in exchange for not putting him back in prison. Dixon had wanted to make the deal, but Ethan had scoffed.

You're being suckered by the Delancey mystique, he'd told him. *As soon as Pereau heard my name, I saw the wheels turning in his brain and the dollar signs in his eyes. Trust me. When you're dealing with the Delancey name there's always a story. A few years ago a murderer tried to get immunity by telling my brother Lucas who really killed our granddad. A couple of times a year the local tabloids will carry a photo that "proves" that Con Delancey is alive and living with a Cajun woman in the bayou or something just as outrageous.*

Dixon had heard the stories himself, so he figured Ethan was right. Still, he hadn't wanted to take a chance. Poor T-Bo Pereau had gone back to Angola, but Dixon had quietly called in a favor and gotten him a few perks in exchange for what he knew about Rosemary Delancey.

T-Bo's information had been disappointing to say the least. All he'd given Dixon was a weak story about seeing a woman who'd looked like the murdered Carnival Queen catching the Prytania streetcar on Canal. When Dixon asked him how he could be sure it was Rosemary Delancey, T-Bo had replied, *Everybody knows the Delanceys.*

Dixon had figured he could write off his time and the favor he'd called in.

But now, as Dixon watched the woman walking down the street, he sent up thanks that he'd followed up on the two-bit dealer's story.

Her hair was inky black and captured into a long, loose braid. She was covered from neck to fingertips to toes by a long skirt, a gauzy long-sleeved blouse and some kind of lacy gloves. But there was no mistaking that tilt of her head or that walk.

Dixon unconsciously touched his wallet, where he carried the photo he'd taken from her apartment all those years ago. A deep sadness still weighed on his chest each time he thought about that horrific, bloody crime scene. It had been his first homicide. The upscale Garden District apartment had been drenched in her blood, but Rosemary Delancey's body had never been found.

The woman slowed down, so he did, too, keeping her in sight but not getting too close. She glided along as if the narrow, uneven sidewalk were a beauty pageant runway, cradling a long loaf of French bread like an armful of roses.

Dixon was no expert on beauty pageants or Mardi Gras Carnival queens, but after her murder he'd searched out every photograph and video ever taken of Rosemary Delancey. He'd become an expert on what she looked like and how she walked.

At that moment she turned her head to check the traffic before crossing Prytania Street. When he saw her full-face for the first time, his certainty melted like cotton candy in the rain.

Viewed straight-on, there was something not quite right about her features. Before he had time to figure out what it was, however, she'd turned away again and crossed the street.

She said something to a newspaper kiosk vendor and he laughed. She continued on. At the door of a two-story shotgun house three doors down she produced a key from a hidden pocket in her skirt and unlocked the door.

Dixon's pulse raced. Had he really found Rosemary Delancey? Because T-Bo Pereau's information had her boarding the Prytania streetcar, Dixon had checked the public records of every single resident within a twenty-block radius, without much hope of success. He'd found three people with names similar to Rosemary.

Rosalie Adams, who was eighty-three; Rosemary Marsden, forty-eight, who owned a dress shop on Magazine Street; and Rose Bohème, thirty, whose signature was on Renée Pettitpas's permit renewal for a display space on Jackson Square. Of the three, only Rose Bohème held any promise, although she was too young to be Rosemary Delancey, who would have been thirty-four. Still, it had been a place to start.

Now here he was, standing in front of Renée Pettitpas's address, his head spinning with excitement. If Rose Bohème was Rosemary Delancey…

Dixon looked up at the house. Its chips and peels spoke of several decades of stucco and paint— white, pink, gray and most recently green. In this part of town, the effect of the crumbling layers with old brick peeking through was charming.

Dixon's sister made quite a good living working to achieve the same effect artificially for clients who loved the look but preferred to pay outrageous sums for faux finishing for their Garden District mansions rather than live in this part of town where they could have the real thing. He ought to take a picture for her. She'd go nuts over the rainbow of colors the crumbling layers revealed.

He glanced upward at the creaky weathered sign that read *Maman Renée, Vodun, Potions, Fortunes* in peeling paint. She'd want to steal that, too.

Just as the black-haired woman pushed open the door, a little girl, maybe eight or nine years old, ran up to her.

"Mignon!" the woman cried, leaning down to buss the girl's cheeks. "Here you are, early as usual." She gestured toward the canvas tote dangling from her wrist. "I have a new piece for you to learn today."

"Miss Rose," the little girl said with a shake of her many neatly braided pigtails, "I want to play 'Saints Go Marchin' In.'"

"In good time, *'tite.*" She pushed the door open and let the girl go inside ahead of her. Just as she entered, she turned back and glanced around. Dixon could have sworn her gaze lit on him for an instant before she pushed the door closed.

For a couple of seconds, he stared at the weathered wooden door with its clear-and-red leaded glass insert, his chest contracting as if a giant fist squeezed it. The little girl had called her Rose.

Rose. Thinking of the woman's features, doubt

nagged at him, but he'd come this far. He wasn't about to give up without checking her out.

He looked around. Maman Renée's voodoo shop was one of a row of similar two-story houses.

In a window of the house next door, he saw an elderly man's gnarled, dusty-black fingers push the lace curtains aside, then quickly let them drop.

The house on the other side and the duplex across the street were both boarded up and the duplex's roof was caved in. They looked as though they hadn't been touched since Katrina.

Half a block up the street, he saw the tables and chairs of an outdoor café. The sign said *Bing's, since 1972.* He walked over and sat. When a husky man with a towel slung over his shoulder and a marine tattoo came out to take his order, Dixon nodded toward the voodoo shop.

"What happened to Maman Renée?" he asked casually, but the man wasn't fooled. He eyed him suspiciously.

"You a cop?"

Dixon gave a short laugh and shook his head. "Café au lait," he said. So Bing was protective of Rose Bohème. Dixon had seen it a lot in the old neighborhoods during his career as a homicide detective. He was glad she had neighbors who cared for her, but it was going to make his job a lot harder if none of them would give him any information.

He'd asked his question about Maman Renée as an icebreaker. He knew that five months ago, Renée Pettitpas, seventy-eight years old, had suffered a stroke. Rose had called 911, but by the time the EMTs arrived, Renée had died.

So what now, Lloyd? he asked himself as he waited for his coffee. The little girl was there for a piano lesson. It fit. Rosemary Delancey had majored in music at Loyola University's College of Music and Fine Arts. Everything about Rose Bohème fit, except her face and her age.

As he frowned, trying to figure out what was wrong with her features, the folded photo in his wallet that he'd taken from Rosemary Delancey's apartment seared his buttock like a brand. He'd always hoped that one day, if she'd survived that bloodbath, someone would see her and recognize her, although truthfully, he'd never really believed the day would come. Yet here he was, about to confront the woman who everyone believed had been murdered twelve years before.

He unwrapped the cloth napkin from around a fork and spoon. The flatware rattled. He held up his hand. He was actually shaking.

Bing returned at that moment with his café au lait. He set it down, then folded his arms and watched him.

sipped the hot milk-laced coffee.

"Why're you so interested in Maman Renée?" Bing finally asked gruffly.

Dixon didn't answer directly. "I see you've been here since 1972."

Bing looked down his crooked nose at him.

He nodded at the tattoo on the man's forearm. "Marines," he said.

"Yeah?"

"I'll bet you can take care of yourself." Dixon watched Bing.

A dark brow shot up. "Wanna try me?"

Dixon shook his head with a short laugh. "No. I guess the folks around here take care of Rose, now that Maman Renée is gone."

"How's any of that your business?" Bing said, unfolding his arms and clenching his fists. "'Cause we don't like questions and we sure as hell don't like cops."

Dixon leaned forward and put his elbows on the table. "I'm worried that Rose could be in danger," he murmured.

Bing stiffened and his eyes narrowed. "How?" he asked.

Dixon took a calculated risk. "You remember when she first showed up here twelve years ago?"

The Marine didn't respond.

"Someone had tried to kill her. Maman Renée took care of her." Dixon watched Bing's expression.

"So you say," the man responded, shru

Dixon studied Bing as he finished his coffee. "You're here every day?" he asked.

"That's right," Bing said forcefully. "And I keep an eye on things, too."

"I could use your help, watching out for Rose," Dixon said. "I can't be here all the time."

Bing's expression didn't soften one bit. "You say a lot, mister, but you ain't said who you are or why Rose is your business."

Dixon stood and slid a five-dollar bill under the empty mug. "I'm a cop, just like you figured. Detective Dixon Lloyd, Homicide." He took out his wallet and showed Bing his badge. "But I'm working undercover. Nobody—*nobody*—can know I'm on the job. Rose's safety is at stake."

"Then why're you telling me?"

"Because you protected her. As soon as I asked you about Maman Renée, you made me as a cop and you wouldn't tell me anything. Can I count on you to keep an eye on her and let me know if you see anyone or anything suspicious?"

Bing nodded. They exchanged phone numbers and Dixon held out his hand.

Bing eyed it suspiciously. "I'm gonna watch out for Rose. I do anyway. And I'll call you if I see anything. But I swear, Lloyd, if you put her in harm's way, you'll answer to me."

"Understood," Dixon said.

Bing eyed him for another couple of seconds, then he shook his hand.

Dixon walked back down the street toward Maman Renée's shop. Once her student was gone, he'd knock on the door and ask the questions that had burned inside him for twelve years.

How had she escaped from her attacker? Where had she gone? And why had she never come forward to let her family and the police know she was alive?

Her murder case—Dixon's first homicide—was the only case he'd never managed to solve. In the past twelve years, he'd earned a reputation in NOPD. They called him *The Closer,* and now he finally had the chance to earn the title. Before this week was out, he planned to close the case the press had dubbed The Beauty Queen Murder.

Rose Bohème closed the front door behind Mignon after warning her to go straight home. She smiled to herself. The eight-year-old had been taking piano lessons for only three weeks, and already she could sight-read five easy pieces. If she kept on like that, Rose wouldn't be able to keep up with her for much longer.

As she climbed the wooden staircase to the apartment above, a flash of light from the window blinded her.

She froze in nameless terror as red amorphous afterimages of the flash seared into her brain.

A second later, rationality overcame the fear. She took a long, slow breath and glanced toward the uncurtained front window. Something metallic, maybe just the foil from a cigarette package or gum wrapper, had caught the late-afternoon sun.

She could hear Maman's voice in her head, chiding her. *Breathe easy,* ma 'tite. *Just forget all that's gone before. Maman put a spell on this house, keep you safe.*

But behind the sweet memory of Maman's voice lurked other unsettling voices, scurrying around the back of her mind with susurrus whispers that haunted her dreams.

Rissshhhh, rozzzzzsss. She pressed her fingers against her suddenly pounding temple and shook her head.

Stop it. Rose closed her eyes and listened for Maman's soothing words again, but the ghostly hissing drowned out all other sound.

Rissshhhh, rozzzzzsss. Rissshhhh, rozzzzzsss.

Pain throbbed in rhythm with the voices. Pressing her fingers against her temple seemed to help. As she massaged the sore place near her hairline, her stomach rumbled.

Of course. She was hungry. That was all that was wrong with her. She hadn't eaten at all today. She thought about the gumbo she'd made this morning. That's what she needed. A big bowl of gumbo and some of the French bread she'd bought. Then she'd go to bed so she could get an early start tomorrow.

Just as she headed back up the stairs, a knock at the door made her jump.

Mignon? Surely not. She should have made it home by now. Rose retraced her steps, squinting against the sunlight, and flipped the light switch near the bottom of the stairs. She unlocked the door, leaving the chain on.

"Mignon?" she started before she saw the looming shadow of the man who stepped forward. "Oh," she said, then, "the shop is closed."

"Hold it." He stuck his foot between the door and the facing as a glint of light on metal flashed in her eyes.

She recoiled with a cry before she realized that the shiny object he held was a badge.

"New Orleans Police, ma'am," the man said in a low, gruff voice.

"Police?" She put a hand to her racing heart. "Has something happened to Mignon?" she rasped.

"No, ma'am," he said. "I'm Detective Lloyd. Dixon Lloyd. I need to ask you some questions."

Rose opened the door to the maximum width allowed by the chain and looked up at him. He was tall, three or four inches taller than her five feet eight inches. His eyes were hooded.

The badge he held reflected the waning sunlight off its burnished surface.

Rose blocked the reflection with her hand, wishing he would put the thing away. What could the police want with her? She hadn't done anything, had she? "I'm sure you have the wrong address," she said.

"No. I have the right address. You are Rose Bohème, right?" His voice was firm, commanding.

He knew her name. Oh, this was not good. "Yes," she said, working for just the right tone of mild interest and slight impatience. "What is this about?"

"Could I come in, please?" he asked, only it didn't really sound like a request. The commanding tone was still there.

"Of course." She tried to keep the stress out of her voice as she unlatched the chain and held the door open. He stepped past her into the foyer, filling it up with his height and his broad shoulders. He brought with him the smell of sunlight, wind and the street.

She sent a glance up and down the sidewalks. Curtains fluttered and a couple of doors slammed shut. She smiled wryly as she closed the door but left it unlocked. People on this end of Prytania

Street didn't like cops. She'd have a lot of questions to answer tomorrow.

"What can I do for you, Detective?" she asked, studying his shadowed face and wishing she'd replaced the second bulb in the foyer fixture. The single pale globe did little more than create eerie shadows along the dusty, bottle-lined shelves and counters of Maman's shop.

The detective didn't answer her. His head turned as he checked around him. Rose didn't like the imperious way he took in the entire room with one sweeping glance and then dismissed it. The only thing that seemed to catch his attention was the stairs. His head tilted as he looked up to the top of them.

"Is there somewhere we can sit?" he asked.

Rose considered saying no. He'd dismissed Maman's shop as beneath his notice, so she didn't feel the need to be even nominally polite. As she opened her mouth to speak, he turned his dark eyes to meet hers.

She looked away. The throbbing in her head increased, flaring into a hot, bright pain. Her personal warning system. This detective wasn't here to ask about some crime or other that had happened in the neighborhood.

He was here for *her*.

So this was it—the day Rose had dreaded for

ever since she could remember. The police had come for her and she had no idea why.

Her entire body tensed as awful, encompassing fear blanketed her. She felt helpless and lost, like she had twelve years ago when she'd woken up to stare blankly at a wizened woman who was wrapping her cuts in soft white bandages.

It took all her strength not to bolt past Detective Lloyd out the door. She clenched her fists and the skin of the scar that ran along her hairline and down her cheek stretched as she frowned. She consciously relaxed her features until she could no longer feel her skin drawing.

"It's okay," he said, watching her closely. "We can talk standing here if you'd rather not allow me upstairs."

His tone worried her and those eyes were positively searing. Was she acting suspiciously? "No, no. Please, come in."

She ascended the stairs, conscious of his heavier, masculine footsteps, his eyes boring into her back and his thoughts, which of course she couldn't read, swirling around her. At least that's how she imagined them.

At the top of the stairs she stepped aside and turned on the landing light. Then she led the way into Maman's living room, where the curtains were open and the waning sunlight was brighter than downstairs.

The detective stopped in the doorway and surveyed the room before he entered. Rose squirmed as she looked at the furniture through his eyes. The green velvet chairs and the old burgundy brocade couch looked threadbare, not fit even for Goodwill. Its frame was in good shape, though, sturdy.

The grand piano's gloss was dazzling under the light, but big and little finger smudges marred the surface.

Fingerprints. Her hands began to tremble. She tried to relax them, but despite her effort they clenched into fists. Her gaze darted back to the piano. Her gloves were there, where she'd removed them for Mignon's lesson.

"P-please sit," she said unsteadily, unwrapping her fingers and gesturing toward the couch. She walked over to the piano and picked up the black lace fingerless gloves and slipped them on as unobtrusively as she could. She perched on the edge of the piano bench and clasped her hands in her lap.

The detective sat down on a chair and turned it to face the piano bench. Then he leaned forward and propped his elbows on his knees, which were mere inches from hers. He sat there, saying nothing, his gaze on her hands—her gloves. It took all her strength not to hide them behind her back like a child.

After what seemed like an eternity, he shifted his gaze to his badge, regarding it as if he'd forgotten he was still holding it. He tucked it into the inside pocket of his jacket.

Rose tried to concentrate on studying him instead of wondering what he was thinking about her. She noticed what she hadn't seen at the door or in the dim light of the shop downstairs.

Detective Lloyd was very well-dressed. Her interest piqued, she assessed him with the eye of an experienced fortune-teller. Maman had taught her that understanding people was all in the subtle details. Rose had a feeling that knowing as much as possible about this detective might be a good idea.

His clothes weren't expensive, but he wore them well. His broad, straight shoulders told her he was proud and confident. A large watch that must have cost a significant portion of his salary rode across his left wrist, its face canted toward his thumb. No wasted effort. He could glance at its face without having to stop and cock his wrist.

His brilliant white shirt was long-sleeved, its cuffs shot perfectly beneath the lightweight sport coat. One edge of his right cuff was beginning to fray. He was frugal, or at least not wasteful, but a faint crease across the shirtfront indicated that he didn't bother with washing his clothes. He had them laundered and folded.

He appeared lean and hard. His thighs were long and lean beneath the dress pants.

His hands were nice. Large and well-shaped, with long, spatulate fingers and short, clean nails. According to Maman, those types of fingers indicated a pragmatic and dedicated person who viewed their work as their top priority. That fit with what she'd already gleaned from his appearance.

The watch was his only accessory and his only indulgence. He didn't even wear a ring. She stared at the fourth finger on his left hand, shifting slightly so that the light caught it at a different angle. Nope. As far as she could tell, he'd never worn a wedding band.

"Ma'am?"

She forced her gaze away from his hands and looked at him, with what she hoped was polite but mild curiosity.

"As I said, I'm looking into an unsolved murder case from several years ago." He fished a small notepad and a pen out of his inside jacket pocket.

"An—unsolved murder?" she rasped. "Whose?"

He didn't answer. Instead, he opened the pad and studied a page for a few seconds. Then he raised his head and fixed her with that dark, sharp gaze. "Now, is it true that you call yourself Rose Bohème?"

Chapter Two

You call yourself Rose Bohème.

The words sent fear twisting in her gut like a knife blade. *Stop it,* she told herself. *Stop thinking about sharp, shiny, deadly things.* A shudder quaked through her.

"Rose Bohème," he said again, his tone suggesting that he didn't believe it was her real name. "How do you spell that exactly?"

She met his gaze and lifted her chin. Suddenly she felt mean. He'd barged into her home without an explanation and dismissed Maman's little shop as beneath his notice. She added arrogant and overbearing to his list of attributes. He didn't deserve a straight answer.

"R-O-S-E," she said sweetly.

His left brow shot up and a dark glint sparked in his eyes. "Thank you. Now your last name," he said evenly.

She bit her lip. He was smooth. "Bohème. B-O-H-E-M-E."

Detective Lloyd wrote on his notepad. "Like gypsy," he muttered.

"That's right," she said, shifting on her perch. "You had questions for me? I'm sure I don't know anything about an old murder."

The detective gave her an odd, knowing look. Did he think she was lying? "How long have you lived here?" he asked.

"More than ten years." Rose crossed her arms. "Was the murder in this neighborhood? Because the only killing I recall was when Gilbert Carven shot a burglar who'd climbed in his window, but that was—"

Detective Lloyd waved a hand. "Please, let me ask the questions. I noticed the sign out front. Is Maman Renée here?"

"No," she said, blinking against the sudden, familiar sting of tears at the back of her eyes. "She died five months ago."

"Sorry for your loss."

The stock phrase uttered in a monotone made Rose angry and dried up her tears instantaneously. "How kind of you," she said icily.

He looked up from his notebook. "I know it can be hard when you lose someone close. Exactly what relation was she to you?"

She hadn't expected that question. Here in the neighborhood, everyone knew them. She didn't recall anyone ever asking her or Maman about their actual relationship.

"She was my...my..." She stopped. She couldn't say *mother*. That was too easily checked. So was *aunt*. "...cousin," she finally said, wincing at how weak her answer was.

"Your cousin," Lloyd repeated sarcastically.

"Once removed on my...my mother's side," she embellished lamely, then bit her lip. She shouldn't have said *mother*. *Don't ask me my mother's name,* she begged silently.

"The house is still listed in her name."

Rose's shoulders hunched as her muscles drew in protectively. This supercilious detective had a habit of stating facts in a way that made her defensive.

Why was he asking about her and Maman? The last thing she wanted was to have the police delving into why she hadn't done anything about Maman's will.

"I fail to see how that has anything to do with an old murder," Rose said archly.

"Is there some reason you think it does?" the detective shot back.

Okay, that did it. She didn't like Detective Lloyd at all. He was pompous and rude. He hadn't even tried to hide his distaste of Maman's quaint little shop. Now he was ignoring her questions. Well, if he wasn't going to answer hers, why should she answer his?

She stood. "I'm not sure how I can help you, Detective. Your questions are awfully intrusive, considering that they can't possibly have anything to do with the murder you say you're investigating. Now, I'm busy, *if* you don't mind."

"Actually I do," he said, looking up at her. He relaxed more deeply into the couch. "I have only a couple more questions."

Rose stood there, arms crossed, staring at him. His hair was black, so shiny it looked blue under the overhead light. From this angle she could tell that his eyes were blue—a deep, almost navy blue. She'd never seen eyes like that before. She tried to remember if Maman had ever talked about what kind of person had navy blue eyes.

"Ms. Bohème?"

She blinked. "What?"

"I said, why don't you sit down? I won't be much longer."

"I'll stand, thank you." She turned toward the window, giving him her profile.

From the corner of her eye she saw him shrug and lean back against the couch cushions. "Fine. Does the name Rosemary Delancey mean anything to you?"

Delancey? Shock sizzled through her, down to her fingers and toes. The painful throbbing in her temple flared again and the susurrus voices that were always there in the back of her brain rose in volume.

Rissshhhh, rozzzzzsss. Rissshhhh, rozzzzzsss, RISSSHHHH ROZZZZZSSS! The words reverberated inside Rose's head, keeping perfect time with the throbbing in her temple. She squeezed her eyes shut.

What had he asked? Something about Delancey.

His hand touched hers. She jumped and jerked away. How had he gotten so close to her without her hearing or seeing him?

"Ma'am?" he said. "Have you ever heard the name Rosemary Delancey?"

"No," she snapped hoarsely. "Never."

She hadn't. So why were the voices bothering her? And why did her pulse throb in her throat as if she were lying?

Detective Dixon Lloyd's gaze burned against her closed lids. "No? Are you telling me you don't recognize the Delancey name?" he asked, the tone of his voice demanding that she open her eyes.

"Well, y-yes," she stammered. "Of course I recognize the name. Everyone in Louisiana knows about Con Delancey. But I don't…I don't *know* any of them." She peered up at him. "Should I? Was it a Delancey who was murdered?"

"Yes," he said, still holding her gaze.

"But…" She was having trouble focusing her

thoughts. The voices were getting louder, loud enough to drown out all other sound. She rubbed her temple and grimaced.

"What about Lyndon Banker?"

She frowned. "Banker? What?" She had no idea what he'd said.

"The name Lyndon Banker. Do you recognize it?"

Rissshhhh, rozzzzzsss. Rissshhhh, rozzzzzsss.

"Are you all right?"

His words barely rose above the hissing in her head. She pressed the heels of her hands against her temples and squeezed. It seemed to help.

After a moment, she answered him. "Yes, I'm fine. What did you say about a bank?"

"Forget that." He dismissed it with a wave of his hand.

Her eyes followed the bright metal of his watch. She noticed that it stayed in place on his wrist.

"Are you sure you don't remember anything about a murder?"

"The murder happened around here?"

"Actually, it happened just off St. Charles Avenue in the Garden District, about six blocks from here. Twelve years ago."

"Twelve..." The vision of Maman unwinding blood-soaked bandages assaulted her.

"Where were you twelve years ago?"

Rose turned her back on him and walked over

to the window, looking out onto Prytania Street. She saw the old neon signs, the flickering lights from the curtained windows, the shadows on the window shades. Her neighbors, her friends.

She loved this neighborhood, this house. It was home. She hugged herself. "I was here," she murmured. "With Maman. I was safe."

She felt the detective's burning gaze on her back. She heard his footsteps as he approached. Then she heard the rustling of cloth and felt something—warmth or energy—emanating from his body.

When he spoke, his voice was too close, too quietly intimate. "Are you sure about that?" he asked.

She whirled and almost hit him, he was that close. She tried to step backward but her heel hit the baseboard. She flattened her palms against the wall behind her.

"Sure about what?" she asked. Where she was or if she was safe? "I don't understand these questions. What does any of this have to do with me?" she cried.

"Think about the name. Rosemary Delancey," he said calmly, then leaned close to her ear and whispered, "Rosemary," drawing out the *S*.

Rissshhhh, rozzzzzsss. Rissshhhh, rozzzzzsss. The whispers blended with his voice, swirling around her in a singsong rhythm. "I—don't—know—anything about—Rosemary Delancey," she bit out, suppressing the urge to squeeze her temples between her hands again.

"I think you do," he said, staring down at her. He lifted a hand toward her hair.

She recoiled, alarm rising in her chest. She slid sideways, away from him. "Get away from me," she cried.

He stepped backward, regarding her narrowly. His jaw tensed. "Rosemary," he said. "Say it. Rosemary."

"Stop it!" She squeezed her head again. "I don't know that name. Why are you doing this?" Her temple throbbed again.

"I think you know why," he said quietly.

Rose's temper burst into flame. "Leave me alone! I don't know anything! I never heard of her!"

Detective Lloyd's eyebrows went up. "That's surprising, because she was someone who should have meant a lot to you."

"Why? How?" Rose asked, grabbing the sleeve of his jacket in her fist and shaking it. "Stop playing with me and tell me what you want me to say."

Dixon Lloyd looked down at Rose's hand on his arm. It was a pretty hand, with long slender fingers and short unpainted nails. Nails that didn't go with the image stored in his head, but then, nothing about this woman matched up with the twenty-two-year-old girl he'd come to know.

He focused on the black fingerless lace gloves she'd put on as soon as she'd been able to get to the piano to retrieve them. Were they an affectation, along with the long flowing skirt and blouse? Was she trying to perpetrate a witchlike image, similar to the seventies and eighties pop icon Stevie Nicks? Or was all that gauzy feminine garb hiding something—like knife scars?

The thought surprised him. Then, as he considered it, a queasy anger turned his stomach.

Swallowing against the queasiness, he turned his attention to her face and studied her up close for the first time. Most interesting was a long scar that started at the level of her right brow and traveled jaggedly down her cheek to her jawline. The shriveled skin drew her mouth slightly on the right side and caused her right eye to slant upward.

His stomach turned over. *Scars.* Of course. *That's* why her face seemed off. The photo he'd carried in his wallet all these years was of a pretty girl with good bones and the promise of classic beauty once she matured. She'd been barely twenty-two when she'd died. Disappeared, he corrected himself.

Now the scar, along with the character that came with age, made her face much more interesting. Still lovely. If possible, even more fascinating. Certainly no longer a Stepford beauty queen.

She was stunning. Stunning and mysterious, a dangerous combination.

"—unless you explain," she was saying.

"What?" He'd missed most of what she'd just said.

"What do you mean *what*? Everything. Why you're here. Who Rosemary Delancey is. Why you think any of this has anything to do with me."

She tossed her answer at him as a challenge, but Dixon didn't think she was nearly as brave as her words sounded. Her face was pallid, her eyes were becoming damp and a fine trembling shimmered through her.

He steeled himself against her tears. She'd stayed hidden all this time—why? Because of the scar? He could understand a young debutante not wanting to be seen in public with what must have seemed like a hideous facial deformity.

But Rosemary Delancey was thirty-four now. Was she still so vain? Or was she afraid of whoever had attacked her? Whatever the reason she hadn't come forward, she knew now that the gig was up.

It was time to hit her with the facts and gauge her reaction.

"Okay," he said, holding up one finger. "First, Rosemary Delancey was the victim of a violent attack twelve years ago. She lost so much blood that the medical examiner concluded that she could not have survived. But that conclusion couldn't be verified because her body was never found."

He held up a second finger. "Second, I'm here because someone recognized you."

Rose's amber-colored eyes went wide, whites showing around the iris. Her face drained of color. She pressed a hand against her chest, which rose and fell rapidly. "Recognized me?" she croaked.

Dixon was surprised at her obvious terror. He knew it was real. No one could fake that sudden pallor. But if she was that afraid of being found, why did she live only a few blocks from where she was attacked? Why hadn't she left the city? Or gone back to her family? If anyone could make her feel safe, it was the Delanceys, wasn't it? He filed that question away to think about later.

He continued, holding up a third finger. "Finally, why should it matter to you? I would think that the answer to that question is obvious, *Miss Delancey*."

Her hands flew to her mouth. She moaned. Her face turned from palest pink to sickly green and her eyelids fluttered rapidly. Then her pupils rolled up and she collapsed into his arms.

Dixon caught her barely in time to keep her from crumpling to the floor. He struggled to hold on to her limp body. He'd deliberately baited her, throwing the name at her, and he'd been prepared for an explosive reaction—maybe even a violent one. He wouldn't have been surprised if she'd hit him or tried to run away, but he sure hadn't expected her to faint.

"Hey, Rosemary," he murmured, close to her ear, as he slid his arm around her back to get a better hold on her until he could move her to the couch. "Can you hear me? Are you okay?"

Her limbs went from rag doll–limp to stiff as boards in less than a second. "Let me go," she cried hoarsely, pushing at his biceps and scrambling to her feet.

He wrapped his hands around her upper arms and gave her the once-over to be sure she was actually awake before he loosened his grip.

Immediately, she teetered, but when he reached out to steady her, she threw her palms up and stumbled backward. "I want you out—of here," she demanded breathlessly.

He studied her. She was still pale—her skin looked translucent, but the greenish hue was gone and pink splotches were growing in her cheeks. Her chest rose and fell rapidly.

"Not until I'm sure you're all right."

"Of course I'm not—all right," she exclaimed. "You come—barging in here—making accusations—"

He arched a brow at her choice of words. "Accusations? I'm not accusing you of anything—

yet. I'm a police detective. All I'm doing is asking questions, Miss Delancey."

"Stop calling me that!" she snapped. "Why are you doing this?"

Dixon frowned at her. "I'm trying to get to the truth about what happened the night you were attacked. How did you get away? Why have you never come forward? Never contacted your family to let them know you're alive? Is it because you're afraid of your family?"

Rose gaped at him and her fingertips whitened against the back of the chair. Her other hand brushed at the scar that ran along her hairline and down her cheek. "I don't know what you're talking about."

As he watched her, a seed of doubt took root inside him. What if she was being honest? What if she really didn't know what he was talking about?

What if she really didn't remember?

He didn't believe in amnesia. There were instances where people who had been through a traumatic event might not remember the specifics, but full-blown amnesia—forgetting everything about one's life? Nope, he didn't buy it.

But Rosemary looked completely dumbfounded. Her wide eyes were filled with terror. Could anyone fake that kind of fear?

"Okay, then," he said, more gently than he'd spoken to her yet. "Tell me about Rose Bohème.

Who are you? Where were you born? Where did you go to school? And how did you get that scar?"

Rose jerked her hand away from the side of her head and lifted her chin indignantly. "You have no right..." But her voice faded.

"Rosemary, what happened to you?" he said gently.

Her lips thinned and her eyes glittered with tears. "Please, go away. Please, leave me alone."

"I can't do that. You are Rosemary Delancey, aren't you? Twelve years ago you were attacked in your apartment. Tell me what happened that night."

She blinked, and the tears that had been clinging to her lashes streamed down her cheeks. She shook her head. "I can't. I don't know. I don't—"

"How did you get away from your attacker?"

"Get away?" More tears fell. She swiped at them with trembling hands.

Dixon turned away and paced back and forth. He wasn't by nature a bully, although he could be as tough as he needed to be with reluctant suspects. But he didn't know how much longer he could keep hammering away at this seemingly fragile, terrified woman. He felt like a bully.

He stopped at the window and stared out at the quiet street. If she was acting, her performance was Oscar-worthy. He turned and stared at her for a moment. "Why don't you tell me what you remember?" he asked gently.

She wiped tears away again. She looked at the couch and perched on the cushion's edge, then stood again and wrapped her arms about herself. She looked miserable, cornered.

Dixon had a sudden, unfamiliar urge to go to her, take her hands in his and promise her that everything was going to be all right. He'd comforted victims and families many times, but he'd never wanted to. It had always felt awkward and insincere. He knew—all too well—that a pat on the hand and a *there, there,* was totally useless when someone's life was in tatters.

"You have to go," she muttered, standing there with her fists clenched and her eyes blazing like imperial topaz. "Get out of here."

"Rosemary," he said. "A terrible thing happened to you, but—"

"Get out!" she shrieked, flailing her lace-covered fists. "Get out now! Or I'll call the police!"

"Hey." He put out a hand toward her. When had she gone from terrified to hysterical? "It's okay. Remember I showed you my badge? I'm a police detective."

"I'll do it!" she screamed, her eyes glittering wildly. "I'll call 911. I'll tell them you assaulted me!" She turned toward a table on the opposite side of the room, near the piano, and Dixon saw the telephone there. Her purse was sitting next to it. He beat her to it.

"Okay," he said, holding up his palms. "You've had a shock tonight. I'll leave, for now."

He stayed between her and the telephone as he glanced inside her purse. "But first, I'm going to give you my cell phone number. Okay?" He eyed her carefully.

Her eyes were still wild and her face was unbearably pale except for the pink splotches, but she didn't move as he dug in her purse.

"That's my—" she started, but he silenced her with a gesture.

"All I'm going to do is call my number from your phone. Then you'll have my number and you can call me if you need me, okay?"

She put her fingers to her left temple and rubbed, squinting at him. "I want you to go!" she said, her voice rising again.

"Okay, okay." He touch-dialed his number on her keypad, then hit the stop button once his phone began to ring. "There," he said, pitching his voice low. "Now you have my number and I have yours. Listen to me, Rosema—Rose. Remember my name. It's Dixon. Dixon Lloyd. I'm not here to hurt you. I want to protect you. I want to help you find your way home."

Her face changed so abruptly that Dixon was afraid she was going to faint again. The fear and agitation drained away. Her eyes softened and filled with tears. She pressed her hands together, prayerlike, and touched her fingertips to her lips.

"Find my way home?" she whispered.

Chapter Three

Home. The word from the detective's mouth penetrated like a ray of light into Rose's clouded heart. For an instant, hope blossomed in her chest.

"Home," she mouthed, afraid to actually put voice to the word again, lest saying it might destroy it.

Then she met Dixon Lloyd's gaze and saw a glint of triumph lighten his dark blue eyes. He was playing on her emotions, trying to catch her off guard.

She straightened and lifted her chin. "I am home. I don't want your help and—" she drew in a breath that caught in a sob "—and I don't need your—protection." She crossed her arms. "I want you to *get—out!*"

She dug her short fingernails into her arms and glared at him until he lowered his gaze and dropped her cell phone back into her purse. He looked at her again, started to speak, then apparently thought better of it. He walked past her out of the living room.

His footsteps echoed and faded as he descended the stairs. For a couple of seconds, there was silence. Rose stiffened and held her breath, listening, until she heard the front door open and close. She let out a careful sigh, and winced as the throbbing in her head flared again.

He'd nearly caught her off guard with his clever mention of *home*. But how? Why had the word affected her so? What she'd told him was true, as far as it went. Maman's house was her home. It had been for the past twelve years.

But before that…

Rose closed her eyes against the pulse that beat painfully in her temple. She needed to follow Detective Lloyd and make sure he'd left, then lock the door and put the chain on, but she couldn't face the stairs. The headache was making her feel light-headed. She needed a migraine pill.

She made her way to her bedroom and swallowed a tablet without water. Turning out the light, she lay on the bed in the dark for a few minutes until the pounding in her head ebbed from horrific to nearly bearable.

Finally, shading her eyes with her hand, she forced herself to stand and make her way carefully down the stairs.

When she checked the door, she found that

the detective had thrown the latch. She locked the dead bolt and put the chain on, then slowly climbed the stairs again. She made her way into the kitchen. She fumbled in the cabinet for a box of crackers and grabbed a soda from the refrigerator. She took the food into her bedroom, where she forced herself to eat the crackers and drink a few sips of soda. The chilled cola eased her stomach a bit. She lay down and tried to relax, but she wasn't strong enough to hold the nightmare memories at bay.

Rissshhhh, rozzzzzsss. Rissshhhh, rozzzzzsss. The whispers took eerie, ghost-like form and swirled around her like banshees. Blood fell like rain, washing over her vision and bringing with it the sharp, bright glint of light on slashing metal.

She moaned and covered her head with a pillow.

A long time later, the silvery flashes faded along with the whispers, and Maman's soothing voice slid into her dreams, soothing the pounding in her head and erasing the vision of the slashing, searing knives.

DIXON WALKED AROUND the outside of Rose's home, assuring himself that all of her lights were out. He glanced at his watch. It was only eight-thirty. He waited a few more minutes, to be sure she hadn't turned them out in preparation for going out. But the house remained dark and quiet.

When he'd come down the stairs, he'd expected her to be nipping at his heels, making sure he left. But she hadn't followed. He didn't like that she'd trusted him to leave.

However, because she hadn't followed him, he'd had a couple of seconds to check out the official-looking form he'd noticed on the foyer table when he'd first come in. He'd scanned it quickly, with the help of the high-intensity laser light on his keychain. The form was a permit renewal for a vendor space on St. Ann Street, signed by Rose Bohème.

The name on the form was Renée Pettitpas, but the renewal date was after Maman Renée's death. A thrill ran through him as he realized what he was looking at. He glanced back toward the stairs, then back to the form.

Judging by the diagram, the space appeared to be right in front of the praline shop. Dixon had walked by that small square of land dozens, maybe scores of times in the past twelve years. Had Rose been there every time? How had he not noticed the beautiful black-haired gypsy reading her tarot cards or holding a customer's palm?

He was at once gratified and disappointed that he hadn't sensed her there. Disappointed because he might have been able to close her case years earlier, but gratified that he wasn't so in tune with Rosemary Delancey that he could have actually sensed her presence in the middle of bright, busy Jackson Square.

Now he reluctantly headed for his Dodge Charger. He felt an irritating compulsion to stay all night and watch over her. Her reaction to his questions about her attack had worried him. But when she'd threatened to call 911, he'd been forced to acknowledge that the last thing he wanted was to find himself explaining to local uniformed police why he was harassing her.

And for damn sure he didn't want Ethan to know what he was doing. Rosemary Delancey was his partner's first cousin, and in his family's minds, she'd been dead for twelve years. Dixon didn't want to give them false hope or listen to Ethan telling him how gullible he was to believe a broken-down addict looking to score a few perks in prison.

He was going to need more proof than her terror and his obsession before he turned the Delanceys' lives upside down. He tried not to think about what he was doing to her carefully insulated life.

Glancing back at the house once more, he noticed that the faded sign was rocking slightly in the wind. *Maman Renée, Vodun, Potions, Fortunes.*

Rose had lived here, safely hidden away. It was arrogant to assume that now that he'd found her, she wouldn't be safe without him.

FIFTEEN MINUTES FROM the time he drove away from Renée Pettitpas's two-story shotgun house, Dixon was sitting on the cracked, uneven patio of the home he'd bought out of foreclosure four years ago. He'd finally decided two things at age thirty-two: he wasn't the marrying kind, and renting was like tossing his money into the Mississippi River.

He leaned back in the teak chair and took a sip of the brandy he'd chosen instead of a beer.

He swirled the snifter, admiring its amber color in the reflection of the goldfish pool lights. Amber—the color of Rosemary Delancey's eyes.

He'd stood in front of her less than an hour ago, and yet now, the whole experience almost seemed like a dream. He closed his eyes, trying to conjure up the vision of her at twenty-two. The girl whose image had soaked into his brain like her blood had soaked into the hardwood floor of her apartment. But that innocent, smiling girl no longer existed.

Now all he could see was midnight-black hair, shocking in contrast to her dark red brows, the ugly scar that only made her face more interesting and fascinating, the casual flowing clothes that he was sure Rosemary Delancey, debutante and Carnival Queen, had never even considered wearing.

He shifted in his chair and reached for his wallet.

"No," he said out loud, stopping himself. He

stood and picked up the jar of fish food sitting on the glass-topped table beside him.

"Here you go, Pete, Louie. Remember I told you about Rosemary Delancey?"

Louis Armstrong and Pete Fountain, his goldfish, were much more interested in the food he tossed them than his conversation.

"Come on, Louie, you remember. My first homicide. She was the Carnival Queen?" He took a sip of brandy, trying to forget about the photo in his wallet. He didn't want to look at her twenty-two-year-old face. He was no longer obsessed with that girl anymore. That pretty debutante was dead.

"You ought to see her," he told Louis. "She walks like she's on a runway. Her hair is black as night, but those eyes…" He held up the glass of brandy. "See how the pool lights hit the brandy? That's the exact color of her eyes."

Louis gulped down the last of the food floating on the surface of the pool, turned sideways and gave Dixon a sour look, then headed for deeper water.

Pete was still swimming around, looking for one more morsel. Dixon was pretty sure Pete wouldn't appreciate hearing about Rose Bohème's attributes. She was already jealous of Louis. As if she could hear Dixon's thoughts, Pete flipped her tail and disappeared beneath the philodendron leaves that floated on the pool's surface.

He smiled wryly and finished his brandy. "Don't be jealous, Pete. I doubt you'll have to worry about her. You'll probably never meet her."

His cell phone vibrated in his pocket. His pulse jumped. Could it be Rose calling him? But when he looked at the display, he saw that it was Ethan.

He sighed and answered. "Hey, what's up?" He really didn't want to go out on a job this late. Not when he planned to be up before dawn tomorrow.

"Nothing," Ethan said, and Dixon breathed a sigh of relief.

"I just wanted to double check about the time tomorrow."

"Time?" he echoed as he turned off the pool lights and headed inside.

"Were you asleep?" Ethan asked.

"No. What about the time?"

"The Saints's scrimmage? That you wanted to go to?" Ethan said. "Don't tell me you forgot."

"The—" Dixon stopped. He had forgotten. "Sorry, I can't go," he said. "Something's come up."

Ethan was quiet for a split second. "Something's come up since this *morning?*" he snapped. "What the hell?"

Dixon thought fast. "It's Dee. She needs me to—to move some stuff." He winced. He didn't like lying to his partner, but what was he going to tell him? *I'll be busy chasing down a lead on your dead cousin?* Yeah, that would work.

"Right. Your sister is insisting that you change your plans to help her. That's *so* like Dee," Ethan said flatly. It wasn't a question. It was a very sarcastic, disgusted statement.

"Come on, Ethan. You ought to understand family. Dee didn't insist. She just looked so disappointed." It was a low blow, playing the family card, but Dixon knew it would work with Ethan.

Another second of silence. "Yeah. Fine. I'll see if Harte wants to go."

"Why don't you take that girl you've been dating?" Dixon suggested, hoping to redirect Ethan's ire.

"Why don't you mind your own business?"

Dixon laughed. "Uh-oh. Trouble in paradise. What'd you do? Make her get her own drink?" Ethan had been going out with the daughter of a prominent New Orleans attorney. He'd complained about her being high-maintenance.

"No. I didn't do anything."

"She doesn't like football, does she?"

Ethan muttered a curse word. "If it's not cappuccino or designer shoes, she's not interested. Have fun moving furniture."

"Yeah," Dixon said, and started to hang up, then he thought of something. "Hey, Delancey," he said.

"When your cousin died, she was living in her own apartment, right?"

"Dix, really? More questions about Rosemary? That T-Bo really got under your skin, didn't he?" Ethan sighed. "Yes, she was living in her own apartment. Why?"

"I was wondering if there was any friction between her and her parents. Was that why she left home?"

He heard Ethan sigh. "I have no idea. Anything else?"

"Nope," Dixon said and hung up. He scrubbed a hand down his face as he set the phone on its charging station. Eventually he was going to have to tell Ethan that his cousin Rosemary was alive and living less than six blocks from where she was attacked.

Dixon headed through the kitchen to his bedroom. He needed to get to sleep. It was after ten, and 5:00 a.m. would come way too soon.

Once in bed, he tried to clear his mind so he could fall asleep, but just as he was about to drift off, the vision of the twenty-two-year-old Carnival Queen rose in his inner vision, then slowly, it morphed into the fascinatingly beautiful face of Rose Bohème.

Gone was the pretty debutante who'd haunted him for twelve years. It was Rose Bohème, the woman, who needed him now. He would be there tomorrow, in Jackson Square. And tomorrow he wouldn't miss her. Now that he'd found her, he didn't plan to let her out of his sight until he'd solved the mystery of her apparent return from the dead.

ROSE GOT HER table set up by six o'clock. Today she was thankful that she'd crisscrossed the tiny table's top with ribbons to hold the tarot cards in place. The forecast only foretold a thirty-percent chance of rain, but it was already cloudy and the wind was blowing.

She'd braided her hair this morning, but a braid wasn't going to cut it if the wind kept up, so she tucked the fat coils into a knit beret and anchored it with bobby pins. Over the years she'd learned not to mind having her face exposed. Only a very few rude people and children asked about the scar. The children didn't bother her. She explained to them that she'd had a bad accident many years ago.

Once she got her hair anchored, she pulled her wool knit shawl closer around her. Even in New Orleans, late-October mornings were chilly. She shivered and felt in her skirt pockets for her cold-weather gloves. She slipped them on, thankful that she'd tucked them there the previous weekend.

After her nightmarish night, she was lucky

she'd made it here at all, much less remembered everything.

She rubbed her temple and pushed away the disturbing images from her dreams. Nights were bad enough since Maman had died. She was *not* going to let the visions and the voices intrude upon her days.

At least she'd gotten rid of that rude bully of a detective. Once she'd threatened to call 911, he'd beat feet out the door. It made her wonder if he was really a policeman at all.

An arrow of fear pierced her chest. Dear God, that must be it. He wasn't really a detective. Sure, he'd showed her a badge, but she had no idea whether it had been real or not.

Her hands shook as she pulled the shawl closer around her. Whom had she let into her home? Whom had she allowed past the protective barrier Maman had provided so that Rose could feel safe?

Suddenly, she felt her careful control draining away. The faceless, nameless terror loomed— *rissshhh, rozzzzzsss, rissshhh, rozzzzzsss.* Only it was no longer faceless or nameless. The terror had blue-black hair and deep blue eyes. And its name was Dixon Lloyd.

"Yo, Mama. Hey?"

She jumped at the familiar voice. She blinked and realized she was staring at the tarot cards. She looked up.

It was Diggy Montgomery, a kid who danced on the street corner near her. "You okay?" He made a funny hip-hop gesture with his hands.

"I'm fine," she said, dredging up a smile for him. "I like your hat."

"Yeah." He took it off and twirled it, then seated it back on his head. "I found it over on Canal. Blew off some rich dude's head I bet. Wan' some coffee?"

"I would love some," she said, digging into her skirt pocket. She always gave him five dollars for a large cup of café au lait from the Café du Monde and never asked for change. His mother was a waitress there and she was pretty sure he got the coffee for nothing, but she didn't care. He put sugar in it and brought it to her. That alone was well worth five bucks.

When he returned, he had the coffee plus a small paper bag. "Here you go, Mama. Enjoy."

"Diggy, wait. Take another dollar," she called, but he just executed a flawless circle, doing things with his sneaker-clad feet that she wouldn't have believed could be done. Then he tipped the fedora, gave her a cocky grin and a mock salute, and said, "Naw, sugar. You look cold. Eat yo' beignet. 'S all good."

"Thank you, sir," she said, smiling. "Come back later and I'll read your cards."

He shook his head as he sashayed to his corner,

tossed the hat onto the ground to collect tips and started his moves.

The tourists who were out this early were more interested in their places in line at the Café du Monde than getting their fortunes told, but Rose figured by noon, if it didn't rain, she'd have more business than she could handle. After all, it was the week before Halloween. Between now and the first of the year was her most lucrative time.

DIXON PUT THE hood of his sweatshirt up and huddled in line, waiting for his turn to elbow his way up to the counter and get his café au lait. He wanted to sit down and have a plate of beignets, but he was anxious to find Rosemary.

Coffee in hand, he walked down St. Ann Street, sipping at the hot, sweet brew and trying to look like just another guy hanging out on Jackson Square on a Saturday.

Then he spotted her. She was dealing tarot cards, tucking each one under the ribbons that crisscrossed her table. She had on black knit gloves today—still fingerless, and she handled the cards like a shark.

Was the sight familiar? Had he seen her here before and not recognized her? He couldn't be sure.

Watching her, he realized she wasn't reading the cards so much as her customer. The woman was fortyish, tired-looking and obviously going against her husband's wishes by having her cards read. She kept glancing over to where he leaned against the wrought-iron fence that enclosed the St. Louis Cathedral and the park named for Andrew Jackson, smoking a cigarette and glaring at her.

Periodically, he turned his head and yelled, "Get back over here," at two little boys who seemed determined to feed their popcorn to a seagull.

Dixon was pretty sure even *he* could tell the woman's fortune. She was in for another dozen years at least of taking care of her sons, being bullied by her husband and wishing she had more time to herself. But he doubted Rosemary was giving her such dire predictions.

Sure enough, after Rosemary pointed at several cards and talked seriously for a few minutes, the woman smiled and laid her hand on Rosemary's arm. Rosemary blushed and smiled back, and the woman took out two bills and tucked them under the ribbons, earning her a dark look from the husband.

Dixon sat down on a bench next to a bored-looking punk with a dirty blond ponytail and drained his fast cooling coffee. He didn't stare at Rosemary, but he kept an eye on her, not quite sure exactly what he was doing there. He only knew that it was important to him to be sure she was safe.

For the next three hours, he watched her reading cards and making people happy, judging by their reactions and the money they gave her. Apparently fortune-telling wasn't a bad career, especially if the teller was a beautiful and mysterious gypsy.

Chapter Four

Rose had long since draped her shawl across the back of her chair and exchanged her knit gloves for the black lace ones. The afternoon sun was much warmer than the forecasted seventy degrees.

She smiled and thanked the girl who slipped a twenty beneath the dark green ribbons on her little table. It had been easy to read the girl's cards. She wore a small diamond on her left ring finger and her fiancé stood right beside her drinking an energy drink. The cards had reflected what Rose saw in their faces. They were in love and oblivious to the practicalities of marriage.

As the couple walked down St. Ann, looking at the artwork hanging on the fence that bordered Jackson Square, Rose unpinned the beret and let her braid hang free.

She looked around for Diggy, but he'd apparently taken a break or given up for the afternoon. Blotting sweat from her upper lip, she thought it would be worth that twenty she'd just earned to have him bring her a cold drink.

A shadow blocked the sun and fell across her face. She looked up. It was Dixon Lloyd. The detective—or not.

She gathered up her cards and began shuffling them, ignoring him until he set a cold bottle of water down on her table. It was covered in condensation, chilled drops sliding down the frosty plastic to pool on the table and soak into the dark green ribbons. Rosemary licked her lips.

"Go ahead," he said. "I got it for you."

She wanted to push the proffered bottle away, but her thirst won out over her indignation and yes, even her fear.

"Thank you," she muttered ungratefully as she picked it up and twisted off the top. She drank nearly a third of it, stopping only when the cold threatened to give her a brain freeze.

"You're welcome," he replied, sitting down on the flimsy folding chair opposite her.

She set down the bottle and looked at him. "Are you stalking me?" she asked, proud of herself for her control after last night.

He shrugged. "One person's stalker is another's protector," he said evenly.

Rosemary's pulse raced at his words. "Protector?" she repeated drily, determined not to be afraid of him today. It was daylight and they were surrounded by people. Strangers… But surely if she needed help, at least one of them would come to her rescue. "I don't think so. I think you're trying to scare me. Well, it won't work."

"Tell my fortune," he said, smiling at her.

She had to make a conscious effort to not let her mouth drop open. His smile stunned her. Without it, his dark blue eyes were unreadable. His face was a mask, with sardonically arched brows and a wide mouth that could curve ironically.

But his smile turned his navy eyes into warm blue pools, and his mouth from stern to boyish. She noticed that his nose was straight and short, adding to the boyishness of his face. Along with the smile, it instantly removed at least five years from her estimate of his age.

She frowned at him, feeling the skin stretch along her forehead and cheek. Her hand moved to brush the scar, but she stopped it. "All right," she said reluctantly. "I'll read your cards, but I have to warn you, I don't guarantee happy endings."

His smile stretched wider. "I'll take my chances."

She'd already studied and cataloged him last night, using the tools Maman had taught her. Now she thought about the kind of man she'd judged him to be, and decided that for him, happy little hints of the future wouldn't do. Whether he would admit it or not, his challenge to her was to tell him exactly what she saw inside him. And that she would do.

She dealt the cards, surprised when the Fool turned up in position zero. Something Maman had said not long before she died echoed in her head.

Keep your heart open, 'tite. *When I'm gone, your safety will lie in the hands of the Fool.*

He pointed at the Fool card without touching it. "That's significant, isn't it?"

Rose swallowed and rested the heels of her hands on the edge of the table. "Would you like to read your own fortune?" she asked drily.

He shook his head and waited, but his eyes twinkled. *Twinkled!*

"Every card is significant," she said, starting her usual spiel. "Where they are is as important as what they are. The Fool in position zero indicates that—" she took a breath, wishing she could stop herself "—that you don't have to search any longer. You already have everything you need. You're standing on the threshold of a new life. All you have to do is make use of what you already know. But beware. If you become distracted from your primary goal, you'll fail and lose everything."

She felt his dark gaze on her the whole time she talked, but she couldn't tear her eyes away from the Fool card. She'd wanted to skew his fortune— tell him that he should give up his current obsession, but that wasn't in the cards, and she wasn't able to make herself say anything but exactly what the cards foretold.

She started to gather them up, but he stopped her with his hand. She looked up at him, startled.

"My primary goal—what is it?" He angled his head, indicating the cards.

Rose looked at his large, warm hand on top of hers. Its heat sent warmth flowing through the lace into her skin, up her arm and through her entire body. Warmth and promise. *One person's stalker is another's protector.*

No. If he was the Fool, she'd take her chances on her own. She jerked her arm away. "I can't tell you that. If you don't know—"

He nodded slowly, still holding her gaze. "I know." He took a long breath. "It's you."

Rose recoiled, aghast. "Stop this. I shouldn't have…" She picked up her cards, stacked them quickly and shoved them into her large tote. "I have to go."

He stood. "I'll take you home." He collapsed the folding chair he'd been sitting in and reached for its bag.

"No! No, you won't!" She scrambled up, knocking her table over. She reached for it, but he beat her to it. He scooped it up and folded it.

"Give it to me," she demanded. She took a fortifying breath. "I told you, I'll call the police if you don't leave me alone."

"And I told you, I am the police."

"I don't believe you."

He spread his hands. "You saw my badge. If you don't believe me, then call them." His gaze bore into hers. He was daring her, and she could tell by the look in his eyes that he'd thought about it and decided that she didn't have the nerve.

Damn him, he was right. If she called the police, she'd have to explain why the she didn't have a driver's license or a checking account, and why not only the permit on Jackson Square, but also the house she lived in were in Maman Renée's name. She'd have to explain why there was no birth or tax record anywhere for Rose Bohème.

He studied her for a few seconds, then handed over her tiny table. "I'm not your enemy, Rose. I'm trying to help you."

"Well, you're doing a really bad job of it," she cried, "because I was fine—I was safe and—and happy until you showed up. I don't want or need your help. If you don't leave me alone I swear I'll scream."

Dixon held up his hands and backed away. He walked back to the bench where he'd sat all morning, but it was full, so he stood with his hands in his sweatshirt pockets, watching her.

She quickly gathered up her table and chairs, threw their straps over her shoulders and headed toward Decatur Street. She'd catch the Prytania streetcar at Canal Place.

DIXON WATCHED ROSE rushing away from him. He wanted to kick himself. Why had he asked her to read his fortune? Why had he made those cryptic, suggestive remarks? He'd gotten caught up in her gypsy charm and forgotten his goal for a moment. But from the instant he'd first spotted her on Prytania Street, the sight of her had made him reckless.

He wanted to push her, to force her to acknowledge him, and by acknowledging him, to admit that she needed him.

By the time she'd reached Decatur and was about to turn toward Canal, Dixon noticed the man walking behind her. He recognized the filthy blond ponytail and the bedraggled hoodie with a peeling faded fleur-de-lis on the back. It was the punk who'd been sitting on the other end of his bench this morning.

The truth hit him like a physical blow to his solar plexus. Ponytail had been there for the same reason as Dixon. He was watching Rose, following her.

Dixon began walking briskly toward the creep, staying about half a block behind him. Sure enough, Ponytail didn't hesitate when Rose turned the corner. He stayed half a block behind her.

He might just happen to live in the same direction as she did, but Dixon didn't buy that theory for one instant. He dogged the man's heels, staying far enough back not to be noticed, until Rosemary boarded the streetcar.

Dixon was about a hundred feet behind Ponytail when the skinny punk grabbed onto the rail and swung himself up onto the car's steps just as it pulled away. He turned his head to look at Dixon, flipping his ponytail. Then he grinned.

Dixon had screwed up. He'd figured it out about two seconds before the grungy ponytailed piece of riffraff had grinned at him. He'd known Dixon was behind him. That's why he'd waited until the streetcar took off to jump aboard. The question was, had Ponytail just noticed him behind him, or had he known about Dixon all along, even while they were sitting together on the bench?

Dixon felt sick. Was the punk following her because Dixon had led him to her? In trying to protect her, Dixon may have brought the danger right to her doorstep.

He sprinted back to the parking lot where he'd left his car, cursing softly as he dodged pedestrians and other vehicles.

Three minutes later, he was in one mother of a traffic jam.

"Son of a…" Dixon muttered, craning his neck in a vain effort to see past the car in front of him.

What the hell was the holdup? He'd been in bumper-to-bumper traffic ever since he'd pulled out of the parking lot and turned onto Canal Street.

Then the answer hit his brain. The Saints game. He was stuck in football traffic.

He'd never get to Rose's before the streetcar did. If Ponytail was following Rose to attack her, there was no way Dixon could get there in time to save her.

For the first time in his career, he wished he had a siren in his car. He took advantage of a slight break in traffic to pull over and park in front of a drugstore on Canal. It was probably less than three miles by car to Prytania Street. On foot, he could make it in about six to eight minutes, if he cut through alleys and empty lots.

By the time he reached the streetcar stop, sweating and out of breath, the car was pulling away. He looked down Prytania toward Rose's house and saw her about a block and a half away. Ponytail was nowhere in sight.

Working to control his breathing, he took off after Rose at a brisk walk. Even burdened down with her huge tote and her chair and table carriers slung over her shoulder, she still walked as though she'd just been crowned Miss America.

He quickly closed the distance between them by a half block, but she was almost at her house. He didn't take his eyes off her for an instant. His breathing was beginning to approach normal, so he sped up, wanting to catch up with her before she disappeared inside.

Just about the time she reached the corner of her house, he glimpsed the ponytailed punk sneaking from one alley to the next, behind the houses that faced Prytania.

Within the next second, Ponytail saw him. He bared his teeth—not in a smile this time—glanced toward Rose, who was inserting her key into her front door, then turned tail and ran.

It took Dixon a split second to decide whether to stay with Rose or chase Ponytail. He decided to give chase. Rose had her door open. He knew that once inside, she'd lock the door. On the other hand, this might be his best chance to catch the punk and wring out of him what information he could.

He headed after the punk. Sadly, he'd ridden the three miles to Prytania Street, while Dixon had run it. Plus the kid was probably ten or twelve years younger and at least forty pounds lighter than Dixon's taller, more muscled frame.

Even so, Dixon nearly caught him. But just about the time Dixon was almost close enough to grab the guy's flying ponytail, the punk gave a running leap toward a wire fence and scrambled over it.

Dixon started to leap after him, but as Ponytail

topped the fence, something fell out of his pocket. He looked down and apparently decided it wasn't worth getting caught, then jumped down on the other side and hit the ground running.

Dixon considered climbing the fence and going after him, but decided his effort would be futile. He propped his hands on his knees and panted until he got his breathing under control again. Once he'd recovered, he took out his handkerchief and picked up the disposable cigarette lighter Ponytail had dropped. With any luck at all, there would be fingerprints on the plastic case. From the look of the kid, it was a cinch he was in the system.

ARON WASABE TURNED the rib eye steaks and touched the center of one with his forefinger. "Five minutes," he called out.

His wife, Carol, stood and set her cocktail glass on the wicker side table. "I'll get the wine and the salad and look in on Amy and Jill," she said to their neighbors George and Ann Clampette. Their daughters were watching a movie together and eating pizza. "Finish your drinks."

Wasabe's cell phone vibrated in the pocket of his cargo shorts. Grimacing, he dug it out. It was Wexler. He turned away from the Clampettes to answer.

"Make it fast," he growled.

"The Fulbright kid called me. Said he found the woman and followed her to her house, but a cop had followed him and chased him off."

"A cop? Did he say who?"

"Nope. Said he was tall, maybe mid-thirties, with black hair. Said he caught a glimpse of his detective badge."

Wasabe ground his teeth. There were only two people in the world more obsessed with Rosemary Delancey than Wasabe himself. One was The Boss. The other was "Detective Dixon Lloyd," he muttered.

"Lloyd? Isn't he partners with one of the Delanceys?"

"Yeah," Wasabe growled. Lloyd had worked The Beauty Queen Murder. Wasabe had good instincts, and his instincts told him that it was Lloyd who'd chased Junior Fulbright.

"You know how you told me to keep an eye on that T-Bo Pereau? Well, he just got busted again. He went to Angola, but word is he's sporting some nice privileges. The kind you wouldn't expect a lowlife like him to get."

"What are you thinking?" Wasabe asked.

"I'm thinking he took that info about the girl and gave it to Lloyd's partner, Delancey, in return for some favors."

"Hmm." Wasabe nodded. "Could be." If Pereau had told Delancey and his partner, Dixon Lloyd, about Rosemary, Wasabe could be in danger, from more than one side. Things were moving fast—too fast. He had a lot to do and he needed to get to it. Because he sure didn't want The Boss to find out from anyone but him that she'd been spotted alive.

"What now, Mr. Wasabe?" Wexler asked him.

"Did Junior say he got away from Lloyd?" he asked as he tested the steaks once more with his finger. They were ready to come off the fire. He cradled his cell phone between his ear and shoulder and grabbed the serving platter.

"Says he did."

"What do you think?"

"He said she was unlocking the door of a voodoo shop on Prytania when the cop spotted him."

"Check it out, and see if you can find out who Pereau spilled to. I'll call you."

"What if—"

"I'll. Call. You." Wasabe hung up and carried the platter to the table. He took a deep breath. "Dig in," he said heartily.

"Those beauties look perfect," George said, picking up his fork and knife.

Chapter Five

Rose let the straps of the folding chairs and the big tote drop to the floor. She arched her back and flexed her shoulders as she thought about her day. It had been fairly successful. The morning had started slow, but before the day ended she'd told at least two dozen fortunes. Considering that she told her customers to pay what they thought her tarot reading was worth, she'd done very well. The money she made reading cards was enough to keep her in food and pay the utility bills, barely.

She put her hand on the stair banister, already drooling over the idea of a hot mug of rooibos tea. Once she'd had her tea and relaxed for a few minutes, she planned to head over to Bing's café up the street and use his laptop to research Rosemary Delancey.

It galled her that Detective Lloyd had planted the name in her head, but now that he had, she felt compelled to find out everything she could about the woman who he'd said had disappeared at the exact time her life had begun. A frisson of dread rippled through her. She shook off the eerie feeling and started up the stairs, but a brisk knock on the door stopped her.

She turned. Through the octagonal stained glass inset she could see a distorted figure looming. By his height and the breadth of his shoulders, she knew who it was.

Detective Lloyd. A flurry of emotions swirled in her chest. She recognized irritation and apprehension, but there were others she didn't want to put a name to. She sent a longing glance toward the top of the stairs where hot soothing tea waited for her, then sighed and went to the door.

She flung it open and glared at him. "Fancy you showing up here," she said sarcastically.

Dixon Lloyd's expression was grim. "Do you know that you were followed this afternoon?"

She sent him an arch look. "As a matter of fact, yes."

Dixon's jaw dropped. "You knew about him? Did you see him?"

She huffed out a disgusted breath. "Please," she said, rolling her eyes. "I'm *looking* at the person who's been following me."

"Not me," he grated. "The punk in the ponytail."

Rose's pulse jumped, but she worked at keeping her expression neutral. "I have no idea what you're talking about."

Dixon pushed past her into the foyer and headed up the stairs.

"What are you— Wait." But he paid no attention to her. She had no choice but to follow him. When she got to the top, he was already through the living room door.

"Please, come in," she said wryly as he stepped over to the big window and looked out.

He ignored her sarcasm. "Do you know a scrawny punk with a dirty blond ponytail and bad teeth?"

She shook her head, but he wasn't looking at her. "No."

"Do you remember seeing him today?"

"You mean in the square? No, I don't think so. Who is he? What was he wearing?"

"Ripped, faded jeans and a ragged gray sweatshirt with a Saints logo on the back."

"Well, that narrows it down," she snapped. "Who is he and why do you think he was following me? For that matter, why are *you* following me?"

Dixon glared at her, his dark blue eyes turning a stormy gray. "I told you last night, I'm trying to protect you."

"Look, Mr.—Detective Lloyd. I'm beginning to think the only person I need protection from is you. There's no reason for anyone to follow me." She uttered a short, sharp laugh. "Trust me, I don't have *anything* of value to anyone."

She saw the muscle in his jaw flex. "That's where you're wrong."

He surprised her then by doing something that seemed completely out of character for him. He reached out and caught a strand of hair that had fallen over her face and pushed it back. In doing so his hand brushed the scar at her hairline.

She shivered.

"You have memories. They're locked in here right now," he said, his hand lingering at her temple, "but eventually we'll figure out how to unlock them, so we can catch the person responsible for nearly killing you."

She swatted his hand away. "Nobody is trying to kill me. And nobody was bothering me, either—until you came along." She lifted her chin. "If you don't have anything new to say, please leave. I didn't sleep well last night. I'm tired."

"I think you need to come with me. It's not safe for you to stay here alone."

Rose laughed and shook her head in wonder. "Are you kidding me? You don't really think I'm going to go with you? I've been here alone since Maman died five months ago, *if* you call it alone. I have friends and neighbors on either side of me. Bing lives over his coffee shop up the street, and

I teach piano lessons during the week. I'm actually rarely alone at all."

"Are you sure you've never seen that punk before?"

"No, of course I'm not sure. A punk kid with poor hygiene hanging around Jackson Square? That doesn't exactly eliminate very many people." She spread her hands. "As far as who might have followed me on the streetcar—if he was following me to catch me or attack me or rob me, then why didn't he? I had my hands full and I wasn't exactly moving fast." She shrugged a shoulder.

Dixon shook his head. "That's because I spotted him and chased him off."

"Really? Well, Mr. Detective Lloyd, I'm pretty sure that if you're right, and someone other than you is following me, I can only conclude that you must have led them to me."

To her surprise, Dixon winced and rubbed a hand down his face.

"That's it, isn't it? You're worried that you led this *punk* to me." Her eyes were wide and frightened. "Oh my—it was you, wasn't it? You're the detective who worked that murder. *That's* why you're so obsessed about it."

Dixon swallowed and avoided her gaze. "None of that matters. What matters is that you're in danger. By the time I saw the guy who was following you, he'd seen you at your door. He knows where you live."

Rose stared at him. Everything he said quaked inside her like another thunderclap in the storm that seemed to be gathering over her head.

She couldn't stand to be in the same room with him any longer. She stalked into the kitchen and put the kettle on for tea as she muttered to herself.

"Two days ago I was fine. I was happy." Before *he'd* shown up at her door. "Relatively happy," she amended as she scooped red tea leaves into her teapot.

Now, suddenly, people were stalking her, she wasn't safe in her own home and a tall, disturbingly handsome man had appointed himself her own personal prophet of doom.

The kettle began to whistle, so she grabbed it and moved it off the eye, then carefully poured the hot water over the leaves in the teapot. She didn't hear Dixon approaching over the noise of the kettle, but she felt him near her. She could tell herself all she wanted that having him in her house didn't bother her, but she'd be lying. He filled up the tiny space with his long legs and broad shoulders.

"Do you want some tea?" she asked ungraciously.

"Sure," he said. Then, "You know, there's something about all this that bothers me."

Rose put the lid on the teapot and left it to steep.

She turned around, crossing her arms over her chest. "Really? Just one thing?"

He inclined his head and his dark blue eyes might have twinkled, but before Rose could be sure whether she'd seen a spark, it was gone and his expression turned grim.

"You haven't asked any questions."

She narrowed her gaze. "Of course I have. Lots of them."

He shrugged. "About why I keep bothering you. About who might be following you. Sure. But you haven't shown one tiny sliver of interest in what happened to you—" he stopped "—to Rosemary Delancey."

"Yes, I have," she retorted, too quickly.

He shook his head. "No, you haven't."

To cover her consternation, she lifted the lid of the teapot and sniffed at the steam that rose.

"Is it because you're afraid? Or is it because you don't have to ask. You already know what happened."

"I don't know what you want from me. Do you want me to fall at your feet and beg you to tell me about this—this *woman* who means nothing to me?" A spurt of adrenaline, painful in its intensity, shot through her, causing her limbs to tremble. "Well, I won't. I don't want to know about her. I want you to leave me alone."

"That's not going to happen and you know it."

Rose felt tears pricking her eyes. She did know it. She knew something else, too. No matter what she said to Dixon, she did *not* want him to leave her alone. Not really.

Certainly not now, since she'd read his cards. Her fingers tingled again, just like they had when she'd turned up the Fool card for him. Maman had told her, *When I'm gone, your safety will lie in the hands of the Fool.*

Whether or not she believed Dixon Lloyd, she did believe Maman.

She cleared her throat, then asked, "Lemon or cream?"

"What?"

"In your tea. Lemon or cream?"

"Oh," he said, eyeing the teapot. "Lemon—and ice, if you don't mind."

She took a lemon from a bowl on the counter and cut it into wedges and arranged them on a plate.

"It'll be another minute. It's still steeping," she said. "Do you want sugar or sweetener?"

"Sugar," he said. "Tea's not tea unless it's sweet, right?"

She allowed herself a small smile. "I'm not the one to ask. I eat way too much sugar in everything." As Rose retrieved a mug and a glass from the cabinet, she remembered that she had some snickerdoodles left from the batch she'd made the first of the week for her students.

She got a plate and put some cookies on it and set it in front of Dixon. She poured half the tea into a pitcher and stirred in sugar. After putting ice in the glass, she poured the warm sweet tea over it and handed it to him.

Then she poured hot tea into her mug and added sugar and a dollop of cream.

Dixon took a sip, swirled the glass so the coolness from the ice would distribute evenly, then picked up a lemon wedge. He squeezed it one-handed into his glass, stirred the ice cubes briefly with his finger, then tasted it again. With a tiny nod of approval, he took a long swallow. "Good," he said, licking his lips.

Rose realized she was staring at his mouth. She forced herself to focus on something else. That something else turned out to be his neck, where his Adam's apple bobbed up and down as he swallowed. His neck was strong and long. It curved out to form wide, sturdy shoulders—the kind of shoulders that could carry any burden.

She blinked. *Take your eyes off him,* she told herself. *Now.*

She looked down at her mug, then picked it up and wrapped her hands around it. Its surface was warm but hard. Steam rose from the shiny, dark red liquid—liquid the color of blood.

Her fingers seemed to go numb and she quickly set the mug down on the counter. It rattled as she pushed it away.

"Is something wrong?" Dixon asked.

"Of course something's wrong," she said hoarsely. "You've inserted yourself and your *danger* into my life—why, I don't know. So you can satisfy your quixotic tendencies? Or make yourself feel better about not solving that murder?" To her dismay, tears gathered in her eyes and fell, splashing onto her black lace gloves. She took a long breath that hitched at the top like a sob.

"Rose, I don't mean to—"

She held up her hands, palm out. "Stop. Just stop," she said.

"Okay," she said, squeezing her eyes closed and wringing out hot tears from beneath her lids. "Tell me. It's what you've wanted to do ever since you knocked on my door yesterday."

Dixon eyed her thoughtfully for a moment, then wiped a hand down his face. His lips thinned into a straight, grim line. As eager as he had been, why was he hesitating now?

A frisson of fear slid down her spine. Was the story that horrific? Did the prospect of reliving what had happened to Rosemary Delancey all those years ago affect him that much?

Her pulse skittered with a sudden fight-or-flight reaction. She started to throw her hands out to stop him, to push him away and escape, but instead, her fingers sought the tiny ridge of scar tissue that began at her temple. A deep, undeniable resolve grew inside her.

She needed to hear this. If there was even the smallest chance that Dixon Lloyd held the key to her past, she had to know. No matter how awful his truth was, it could not be as horrific as the cold, blank wall that existed on the other side of that moment when she'd woken up in Maman's gentle care.

She realized Dixon was watching her, a curious expression on his face. When she met his gaze, he blinked, then looked down and traced a drop of condensation down the side of the glass with his finger.

"You're sure?" he asked.

Rose squared her shoulders and lifted her chin. "I'm sure," she said, hoping her voice didn't sound as quavery to his ears as it did to hers.

"Okay." He took a deep breath. "Rosemary Delancey was the oldest grandchild of Con Delancey, the infamous Louisiana politician. She had it all. She was beautiful and wealthy. She was on top of the world. Just a few months before, she'd been Mardi Gras Carnival Queen and had ridden in the parades and reigned over the Ti Malice Ball."

He stopped to take a breath and drain the last of his iced tea.

Rose stared at him. "You certainly know a lot about her. Did you know her?"

He shook his head and his cheeks turned pink. "No," he said on a wry laugh. "I didn't run in her circles. When I got the call that night, I was the very definition of wet-behind-the-ears rookie. Hers was my first homicide case as a detective. It was late—nearly midnight. We were called to an apartment on St. Charles by the superintendent, who was hysterical. He'd gone to check out a complaint of banging and screaming and found the door to the apartment open. When he went in, he saw the blood."

Rose swallowed. Blood. Bloodred. Her brain was hyperaware of the mug on the counter, filled with the bloodred liquid.

"When we got there, we found the apartment covered in blood," Dixon went on, his eyes watching her closely. "The bedclothes. The floors. The bathtub."

"The bathtub?" Rose echoed.

Dixon nodded. "There was a glass of white wine sitting on the edge of the tub. Bloody fingerprints streaked the tiles just below the ledge where it sat." He set his mouth, pressing his lips together. "The water in the tub was pink with blood."

"And—her? Rosemary?" Rose couldn't resist asking, although she already knew the answer.

He shook his head. "Nowhere. All that blood and no body." He set his empty glass on the counter.

Rose stared at it. For an instant her vision wavered and the tumbler morphed into a wineglass, reflecting pink from bloody water. She blinked, trying to rid her brain of that picture. Telling herself that it was her imagination and not a memory.

"Rose?" Dixon touched her hand briefly.

"I'm—I'm fine," she stammered. "I don't drink wine."

He sent her an odd look.

"So you never found her?" she asked, knowing as soon as she opened her mouth that her question was foolish—naive.

"No. Not un…" But he stopped, and let the unspoken words linger in the air.

Rose swallowed against a queasy feeling in her stomach and gestured toward the pitcher of tea. "Do you want some more?"

He shook his head. "The medical examiner said he couldn't tell how much blood had gone down the drain. Blood can be deceiving. A little bit can look like a lot. His opinion was that she'd lost too much blood to survive."

—too much blood to survive. At Dixon's words,

Rose's mouth and throat went dry. So dry she couldn't speak.

"Then we got another call. A body had been discovered—"

Rose gasped. "A body? But…" She stopped at his sharp look.

"It had been dragged behind a Dumpster about four blocks away, shot in the back, twice. The victim was Lyndon Banker, the son of Eldridge Banker—" Dixon met Rose's gaze "—and Rosemary Delancey's fiancé."

Chapter Six

Rose's amber eyes widened and what little color she had in her face drained away. "Fiancé?" Her voice was nothing more than a rasp.

Dixon nodded. "We figured that Banker had come to Rosemary's apartment and had caught the killer in the act. He ran—" Dixon shrugged "—maybe to get the police. The killer followed him and shot him."

"You know that?"

Dixon's eyes narrowed. "Know what?"

"That her fiancé saw the killer."

"We found Banker's footprints in the blood on the hardwood floors, and Rosemary's blood on his shoes."

He was going too fast for her. The players in this macabre little game were becoming confused in her head. "What if it was her fiancé that killed—" not killed "—hurt her, and the other person caught him and shot him?"

"It wasn't. Banker wasn't carrying a knife. Plus,

if he'd done it he'd have been covered with blood, not just the soles of his shoes." He assessed her. "Why would you ask that?"

"I don't know."

His mouth thinned. "Anyhow, after he shot Banker, the killer went back to Rosemary's apartment to dispose of her body."

"Dispose of it? I thought—"

"That's what we figured he'd done, based on his footprints. But she was gone and she's never been found." Dixon's deep blue eyes said what he didn't put into words. *Until now.*

"But…you said according to the medical examiner she couldn't have survived."

"The M.E. said it *appeared* she'd lost too much blood to survive."

Rose shuddered. "I don't understand why you're telling me all this. Why are you so sure I'm this… woman?" She couldn't say the name Rosemary Delancey.

Dixon regarded her solemnly. "It all fits," he said. "The scar on your face. The timeline."

"But you don't know for sure." She rubbed her temple.

It was all too easy to conjure up a picture of the beauty queen's apartment, streaked and smeared with blood, the floor tracked with— "Footprints," she whispered.

"Her footprints were everywhere," he said.

"Bare. Bloody. On the tile, on the hardwood floors. Everywhere."

"And his, right? The killer? What about his?"

Dixon shook his head. "Lyndon Banker's shoes were some kind of ridiculously expensive leather sneakers with the name on the sole. Testini or Testoni or something. The other man's shoes were cheap loafers—nothing unique about the impressions our CSI made except that they were worn down on the left heel. Unidentifiable."

Rose's thoughts were whirling desperately. Panic was tightening around her chest like a vise. "The knife? The gun? Fingerprints? There had to be something."

"This was my first homicide, Rose. And it's the only case I've never been able to close. Trust me, I covered everything. The gun used to kill Lyndon Banker was lying beside him—left there deliberately. It was a .22 with a body already on it, but it was wiped clean. The only bit of trace that CSI managed to get off it was some of Rosemary Delancey's blood embedded in the grip."

"What do you mean 'a body already on it'?"

Dixon waved a hand. "That just means that the gun had been used in the past to kill someone. The bullet from that homicide and the bullet taken from Lyndon Banker's body were a match."

"You didn't find any of his DNA at the crime scene?" Rose croaked as the vise tightened even more. "I mean—she must have struggled. Surely she managed to scratch him or grab his arm or something." She flung her arms wide. "How could there be all that blood all over the place if she didn't fight?"

"I believe she did fight," Dixon said. "I believe she fought with every ounce of breath in her body to stay alive. She probably did scratch him. I hope to hell she did. But with so much of her blood at the scene, it would have taken a miracle for CSI to identify what would have been a minute trace of his, especially back then."

Rose was speechless. None of what Dixon said conjured up a single memory, but her imagination was making up for what her memory lacked. She could picture Rosemary Delancey struggling, scratching, stumbling as she tried to get away from the man's glinting, flashing knife.

The imagined glint of light on steel sent throbbing pain to her temple. She winced and her heart raced. Did she remember a knife? Was that why any sudden flash of light could trigger a migraine? Her fingers found the sore spot and massaged it.

"Are you all right?" Dixon asked.

She nodded, pressing her lips together. "This is just so awful. That poor girl."

Dixon went on. "I don't think the killer intended to kill her. I think he went to her apartment to try and get money out of her. It's my theory that he was sent by someone Banker owed money to—a lot of money. He was a notorious gambling addict. He'd long since run through his own inheritance. It turns out that none of the Delancey heirs could touch their money until they turned twenty-five. I think the killer must have—" Dixon paused for a moment before continuing. "I think a lot of blood was spilled before the killer found that out."

"I don't understand," Rose said automatically, although inside her, a nauseating dread was building. She was afraid she did understand—much too well.

He wiped his hand down his face again and sighed. "I think most of the blood in the apartment was from small cuts, shallow cuts," he explained with a grimace. "If the killer was experienced with a knife, he could spill a lot of blood and cause a lot of pain without endangering his victim's life. Most of the cuts would be minor."

He met her gaze and held it for another long moment. "And a lot of them would have been on her hands and arms—and chest."

Dixon watched Rose's reaction. As he'd expected, she knew exactly where he was going with his comment.

Her eyes widened, then she squeezed her hands into fists, took a step backward and crossed her arms.

Dixon stepped around the kitchen counter. "Let

me see your hands, Rose," he said softly, holding his out, palms up.

She shook her head, her wide amber gaze never wavering from his face. "No."

It wasn't even a word, just a movement of her lips. She took another step backward.

He didn't allow his hands to waver. He kept them out placatingly. "Come on. I told you the truth, Rose. I'll protect you. I swear. Whoever he is, he can't hurt you as long as I'm around."

He moved slightly closer, watching her eyes. He felt as though he was coaxing a half-wild, starving kitten. One wrong move and she would bolt.

Then tears welled in her eyes and rolled down her cheeks, and even while she was still shaking her head, her shoulders slumped and she uncrossed her arms. Without a word she peeled off the lacy gloves and let them drop silently to the floor. Then she pushed the long, flowing sleeves of her blouse up, exposing her forearms.

Dixon held his breath. He'd waited twelve years, his entire career as a New Orleans Police Department detective, for this moment. Although he'd never told a soul, not his partner, not even his sister, he'd never stopped looking for Rosemary Delancey.

But now, with this beautiful, frightened woman

standing in front of him, offering him proof that his search hadn't been in vain, he felt frozen with fear.

A part of him didn't want to see what the face-less, nameless monster had done to her. That bloody apartment had told its horrible, gory tale very well, without Dixon having to lay eyes on the permanent reminders the man had left.

He had to blink before he could focus on her arms and hands. When he did, the first thing that struck him was that the skin was as creamy as her face, a sort of pale peach color. Delicate blue veins traced the inside of her slender wrists.

But her beautiful skin was merely the canvas. The man who had attacked her had used his knife like a mad Pollackesque painter. Thin white scars crisscrossed her forearms and wrists. There were even a few on her palms.

Dixon realized his jaw hurt, he was clamping it so hard. He blinked again and rubbed his eyes, then tried to pretend his fingers didn't come away the least bit damp.

Carefully, gently, he ran his thumbs and fingers across the soft skin. Most of the cuts were so shallow that he couldn't detect the slightest ridge, not even with the sensitive tips of his fingers. He turned her hands over. The tiny, torturous scars were as plentiful on the back as on the front.

Pain seared down his neck and up to his temple. He made a conscious effort to relax his jaw. His gaze slid up her forearms to the bunched sleeves of her blouse, then farther, to her shoulders, and stopped, lingering on her breasts.

He shook his head to rid himself of the image of what the monster must have done to the still-hidden parts of her.

Bending, he picked up her gloves from the floor and handed them to her. He didn't meet her gaze. He couldn't.

He'd pushed her, bullied her, forced her to this point, and now he was filled with shame. He shouldn't have made her expose herself like that. What had been his point?

Not to prove who she was. He didn't need proof. After that first moment of doubt when he'd seen her face full-on just yesterday, he'd known for a fact. He hadn't needed the added proof of the scars on her body.

No. He'd done all this to prove to *her* that she was Rosemary Delancey. Only—he'd expected her to be defiant, like she had been so far.

It broke his heart to see her looking so small and helpless. So defeated.

He turned away.

"Dixon?"

Her voice was small, hesitant. The touch of her

hand on his wrist was tentative. He stopped but didn't turn back.

"It's me, isn't it?"

He winced.

"I'm—" her breath hitched "—I'm Rosemary Delancey."

The words weren't a question; they were a statement. But far more telling than the words was the tone of her voice.

She was consumed with terror. She made a small sound—a quiet, hurt-animal sound. He knew she hadn't uttered it consciously. It was what it sounded like—a soul-deep moan of pain. Not physical. Emotional.

Any last lingering suspicion that had been hidden behind his heart drained out of him. She hadn't known.

He'd never believed in amnesia. But now he had to. He had living, breathing proof.

Without thought, without even meeting her gaze, he turned and pulled her into his arms. He had no idea how to comfort her. He was pretty sure that nothing he did could possibly be enough.

So he just held on to her. He pressed his cheek against her hair and held her against him, feeling the fine trembling that quivered through her whole body. Feeling the warmth of her breath against his neck. Feeling the way her fists bunched the material of his sweatshirt.

He wasn't sure how long they stood there like that, holding on to each other, but eventually the comforting embrace became decidedly uncomfortable—to him.

Her hair smelled like honeysuckle and he found himself not so much resting his cheek against it as nuzzling it. He began to notice the way her back curved, the way her shoulder muscles turned elegantly up to her neck, the way her breasts and belly felt against him.

Suddenly, lust arrowed through him and hit its target dead center. He stirred, hardened. For a moment that seemed to stretch into an eternity, he hovered on a razor's edge, unable to let go of her and unwilling to let her know how she affected him.

While he struggled with himself, her body softened. She lifted her head, just enough that if he lowered his a fraction of an inch, their lips would meet. She slid her hands up until her palms rested against his pecs. Did she know? Did she sense how much he wanted her?

He groaned under his breath and caught her hands in his.

"Dixon?"

He shook his head. "I'm sorry, Rose. I didn't mean to—"

She backed away. "Please don't."

For an instant he thought she was asking him

not to stop. But she pulled her hands away and twisted her fingers together.

"Don't say you're sorry after you've come in here and disrupted my life." She shook her head and her shoulders tightened. "I don't know what to do now. Before yesterday I didn't know who I was or what had happened to me...." She stopped and looked up at him, her gaze hard and fearful at the same time. "But I was happy."

Dixon felt a queasy thud in the pit of his stomach. He set his jaw. "I need to be sure you're safe. Is there somewhere you can go? Someone you can stay with? You shouldn't be here by yourself."

She stiffened visibly. "I'm not going anywhere, Detective," she said haughtily. "This is my home. I have piano students who expect me to be here. You are not going to disrupt my life any more than you already have."

He'd asked Bing to watch her, but could he depend on the café owner? The man certainly cared about Rose, and he was an ex-Marine, but Dixon didn't want to leave Rose's safety in his hands alone. "Why are you being so stubborn?" he snapped. "You know you were followed today. I don't know what that guy might have done if I hadn't scared him off."

"No," she said emphatically. "I *don't* know I was followed. *You* are the only one who saw him.

I didn't. I have dead bolts. I have a cell phone. I have neighbors. I will be fine."

Dixon was so angry that his ears burned. "You have got to be the most stubborn person I have ever met."

She crossed her arms and lifted her chin.

His jaw began to throb because it was clamped so tightly. "I'll assign a cruiser to drive by here every hour from 8:00 p.m. to 6:00 a.m. But I don't like it."

"Don't you dare! That's ridiculous. I don't want someone watching me at all hours. And a police car circling around here all night will spook my neighbors."

"Good. Maybe it'll spook whoever's following you, too," Dixon snapped. "A lot can happen in an hour. I doubt it took the killer an hour to do all that damage." He nodded, indicating her hands and arms.

When her face drained of color and her shoulders drew up, he felt like a heel. "Rose, listen to me—"

"Get out!" she grated through clenched teeth. "Just get out of here."

He got out. Why had he said that? It had been a mean remark, but he'd been at the end of his rope, casting about for some way to force her to acknowledge the danger she was in.

He wanted to turn around and apologize, but he

knew it wouldn't do any good. She was already suspicious of his motives. That remark probably made her hate him. Worse, it had likely destroyed any chance he had of winning her trust.

As HE STRODE up the street to where he'd left his car, he dialed a buddy of his who patrolled in the Garden District, Ray Fieri.

"Hi, Ray," he said. "You still on night shift?"

"I sure am," Ray said. "You want to trade jobs?"

Dixon laughed. "Can I get you to do me a favor, off the record?"

"I don't know. Last time I did you a favor I almost got suspended."

"That's bull and you know it. In fact you got a commendation for actions above and beyond."

"Oh, well that, too."

"I need you to drive by this address every hour or so for the next few days." He gave Ray the address of Rose's house.

"That's Maman Renée's place."

Dixon winced. "Right. Can you do it and not mention it to anybody? If you see anyone lurking around, give me a call on my cell—no matter what time it is."

"Lurking?" Ray said sarcastically.

"Lurking, sneaking, whatever you want to call it," Dixon fired back. "And by the way, bite me."

"No problem. I sure do love Very Old Barton," Ray said, a smile in his voice.

"Very Old Barton. Got it. Remember, don't confront anyone. Just give me a call."

"What's going on with you and Mama Renée's girl? I mean, she's gorgeous, but she's kind of odd."

Dixon frowned. "Nothing's going on. What do you mean 'odd'?"

"She's kind of a recluse. I know she tells fortunes in Jackson Square, but I think that's the only place she ever goes."

"Yeah, maybe," Dixon said noncommittally. "Listen, I can't go into details right now. I'll fill you in once I'm sure everything's okay."

"You got it. When you bring me my whiskey, pick up some wings. We'll watch a ball game."

"Sounds good. Call me if you even smell somebody near that house."

Dixon hung up. Ray was a good man. He'd let him know if he saw anybody. He hoped that hourly drive-bys would be enough.

"Damn it to hell, Rose," he muttered as he got into his car. "How am I going to keep you safe if you won't believe me?"

Chapter Seven

If Detective Dixon Lloyd had dared to show his face today, Rose would have strangled him with her bare hands. She'd hardly slept the night before. The nightmares and the susurrus whispers were worse than ever.

She'd gotten to Jackson Square early this morning, but it had started spitting rain around noon, so she'd decided to spend the afternoon working in Maman's shop, sweeping and dusting and cleaning out stacks of newspapers and magazines. But after about twenty minutes, with the sun shining in the bare shop windows and reflecting off glass and chrome, she'd had to stop.

The glints of light flashing in her face and the red reflections made by the ruby glass in the window panes played havoc with her imagination, plunging her into eerie daylight versions of the horrific nightmare visions. The sunlight stabbed her retinas like knife blades and the red reflections looked like blood on the countertops, the floors, even on her skin.

Finally, she walked up the street to Bing's café. "Hi, Bing. How's everything?"

"Hi, Rose," Bing said when he saw her. "Things are fine around here. How about you? You doing okay?"

She smiled and nodded. "I'm fine. Would you mind if I used your laptop? I just want to search something."

"Sure. No problem at all. Go ahead, I've got to fry some beignets. Want one?"

"Please," she said as she stepped behind the lunch counter and sat at his desk. She brought up a search engine and entered the name Rosemary Delancey. To her surprise, there were thousands of hits. Most of them were references to Mardi Gras and the Krewe parades, but there were a lot of pages about Rosemary. Newspaper articles about the murder, complete with photos of a blood-soaked apartment.

Studio portraits and casual photos of a pretty college-aged girl with red-gold hair. Even a picture of the girl dressed in a sparkling silver evening gown and a gaudy tiara, standing next to an older man wearing a massive jewel-encrusted crown that couldn't possibly be real.

Trying to ignore the photos of the bloody crime scene, Rose studied the girl more closely. She found herself touching the part in her own dyed-black hair where reddish-gold roots peeped out in stark contrast to the black. It was time to color it, she thought idly, as she clicked over to the next page of listings.

She found a website that called itself delancey-dynasty.com. It appeared to be a fan site devoted to the family. There was a family tree, bios of the family members and a page for news and rumors. And scattered through the site were photos of the family.

They certainly were a handsome bunch. And there was a familiarity about them. Was it because they were well-known in the New Orleans area, or because the face she saw in the mirror every day looked like them? She touched the scar at her hairline and let her fingers trace the line of her jaw.

Bing came in to pour a cup of chicory coffee and added hot milk. "Everything okay, Rose?" he asked.

Rose closed the browser window. "Fine. I appreciate it."

"Anytime, sugar. You know you can ask me for anything." He set the coffee on a tray along with a plate of beignets dusted with powdered sugar and headed out to deliver it to the customer.

Rose stepped around the lunch counter as he came back inside. "Are you really busy?" she asked.

"Nope, not until somebody wants a refill on their coffee. You want some?"

"No, thanks." She drew in a deep breath. "Bing, do you remember when I—when I came here?"

Bing snapped the dish towel off his shoulder and began polishing the counter. "I guess so," he said. "That was quite a few years ago."

Rose heard the note of caution in his voice. "Maman told you not to talk to me about it, didn't she?"

Bing didn't answer. He reached under the counter for a plastic gallon bottle and poured liquid on the Formica countertop and kept polishing.

Rose smelled the distinctive odor of alcohol.

"It's okay, Bing. I know she was just trying to protect me. But she's gone now and I need you to tell me anything you know about me."

"That cop was here asking questions about you the other day. I didn't tell him anything." Bing slung the towel back over his shoulder. He propped on the edge of the counter stool and crossed his arms. "He asked me to look out for you."

"I need to know," she said simply.

Bing sighed. "The place was open for dinner back then. I guess it's been twelve years now. I don't know how I did it. By the time I closed at nine o'clock, cleaned up and made up the beignet dough so it could rise, it was after midnight. Then I was up at five to get ready for breakfast."

He smiled. "That was before I married Angelique and she made me stop serving dinner."

"Angelique *is* an angel," Rose said.

"Anyhow, Maman called me and told me to bring her a white tablecloth and all the alcohol I had."

Maman unwinding blood-soaked bandages from her hands and arms.

"While I tore the cloth into strips, she told me she'd gone out at midnight to gather dandelion greens. Best time, she said, because the leaves are fat and crisp. She said you were walking barefoot, with a bloody terry cloth robe hanging around your shoulders and whispering something that sounded like *Irish rose*. She said you were covered with blood."

Rose pressed her hand over her heart, trying to calm its erratic beating. "What did I look like?" she asked.

"Can't tell you that," Bing said. "Maman wouldn't let me see you. And she made me promise I wouldn't say anything. Said she'd be telling me the story when she told everyone else."

A couple walked up and sat at a table. Bing took their order and served them while Rose waited. When he came back to the counter, he said, "Where was I?"

"Maman's story."

"Right. She said you were a relative who was

hiding from an abusive boyfriend, and that was it. I doubt anybody ever questioned her. She had a way about her."

Rose laughed quietly and massaged the scar at her hairline. "Yes, she did. You reminded me of something. One of the first things I remember is her telling me that I'd been very sick. She said I shouldn't go outside until I was completely recovered." Rose shook her head. "She had me exercising inside the house every day, but she didn't let me go outside for a long time."

"A few months anyway," Bing agreed. "By the time people started seeing you out and about, it seemed like you'd always been part of the neighborhood."

"Did she know, Bing? Who I was?"

Bing looked at her somberly. "She saw the newspapers of course, just like I did. But the one time I mentioned it to her she shut me up right quick. And of course," he made a slight gesture toward her hair, "when I saw you for the first time, you had black hair."

"Was that why she named me Rose?"

Bing looked out the front of the restaurant but he wasn't checking on his patrons. He seemed to be staring back into the past. "Maman Renée told me once that when she found you, you didn't talk for days, just whimpered and slept. Said she kept asking you who you were—what your name was, but you would just cry. Then one morning she brought you a rose with your breakfast tray and you burst into tears and whispered *rose*."

He started to say something else, then stopped.

Rose waited, her heart in her throat.

"Maman Renée had a daughter. Beautiful girl. She was training to be a concert pianist. Twenty-five years ago, when she was twenty, she was killed by her boyfriend."

"Oh…" Rose was shocked and anguish ripped through her heart like a razor blade. "She never told me."

"She never talked about her. Ever. But then she found you." Bing nodded slowly and raised his gaze to hers. "Yeah," he said. "She knew you were Rosemary Delancey."

WAS IT ROSEMARY Delancey? Wasabe had just pulled up to the curb on Prytania Street when he spotted her walking toward the voodoo shop. He held his breath and angled his head this way and that, but before he could get a good look at her face, she'd unlocked the door to the voodoo shop and gone inside.

Cursing softly, he checked his watch. After six. It would be dark before long. He was going to have to ditch his car and hide somewhere close in hope that he could get a good straight-on view of her face before dusk. If he couldn't he'd be forced to hide—maybe all night. Because now that he was here, there was no way in hell he was leaving until he had the answers he wanted.

He'd borrowed his cousin's beat-up Malibu for the excursion, knowing that his high-end mid-size sedan would stick out like a sore thumb on this end of Prytania. He drove the Malibu a few blocks away and walked back to the house across the street from the shop. He hid in the alley behind the ruined duplex as he looked around for a breach in one of the walls. He couldn't find even one missing nail. The house was tight.

That settled that. It was too dangerous for him to hang around here in the daytime. It would not be a good idea to run into Detective Lloyd, and if Wasabe was right, it would be inevitable. He was sure the detective was stuck to Rosemary like glue.

He'd have to wait until dark. He headed back to his car to wait.

His plan was threefold. He'd come here to satisfy himself that she was Rosemary Delancey. He'd hoped to walk past her, giving her a chance to see his face. He wanted to know if she recognized him. And he wanted to know for certain if the cop was Dixon Lloyd.

While he waited, he looked around the trash bin that was the inside of his cousin's car. There were empty cigarette packs tossed into the passenger seat, along with water bottles and a few fast-food bags, their smell mingling with the stale cigarette smoke with nauseating results.

Wasabe craned his neck to look in the backseat. On the floorboard behind the passenger seat was a massive pile of matchbooks. Wasabe glanced at his watch. It would be at least two hours before it would be dark enough for him to sneak over and spy on the woman through her windows. He picked up a handful of matchbooks and idly looked through them to pass the time.

In less than a half hour, he'd happened upon a gold mine. A matchbook from Doll's Diner in Angola, Louisiana. Wasabe flipped the cover of the matchbook back and forth with his index finger as he thought.

He stuck the matchbook into his pocket and spent the next few minutes searching through the trash in the car. Finally, he found what he was looking for. A nearly empty pack of cigarettes.

He could spook Rosemary, if he decided it really was her, by lighting cigarettes and letting the matches cast flickering, grotesque shadows and highlights on his face. He was pretty sure that if he scared her enough, she'd call Lloyd.

Dixon Lloyd was a good detective. Wasabe pocketed the cigarettes alongside the matchbook and smiled. Lloyd would get the message. Wasabe could get inside Angola if he wanted to.

IT WAS DARK when Rose finally looked up from the piano keyboard. The only light in the living room came from the lamp sitting on the piano. She'd played for hours.

For a few moments she sat there with her fingers poised over the keyboard. When she'd come back from Bing's, she'd felt deceived and betrayed. Maman had kept so many secrets from her. Most of her secrets and *all* of Rose's. The wizened woman was the only family Rose remembered, and yet she'd lied to her for twelve years. She'd kept her from her family. Possibly destroyed any chance Rose had of ever recovering her memory.

As soon as she'd come back from Bing's, Rose had run upstairs and looked around Maman's bedroom. She'd glanced at the massive wardrobe where Maman had kept her clothes, but she knew what was in there. She'd been through it. But the closet—Rose had never been in Maman's closet. In fact, ever since Rose could remember, its door had been locked.

She'd recalled the keys in the back of the flatware drawer. In the kitchen, she'd jerked the drawer open. There, behind the stained and worn silver plate flatware was an old key ring. Grabbing it, Rose had hurried back into Maman's bedroom. She'd tried keys until one turned the lock.

Pulling in a deep breath and sending a silent apology to Maman, she'd opened the door—and stared. The closet was practically empty. There were a few things hanging on hangers, most notably a moth-eaten fur coat. But the only other thing in the closet was a white cardboard box, the kind a gift from a department store might come in.

Rose had pulled the large oblong box from the closet and set it on the floor, then, holding her breath, she'd opened it.

And found exactly what she'd been looking for. She'd stared at the contents of the box for several minutes, her brain racing—not with memories, but again, with her runaway imagination.

Finally she'd reached in and picked up the dark-stained white terry cloth robe. "Oh, Maman," she'd whispered in a strangled sob, "why didn't you tell me?"

She looked at her fingers, still poised over the ivory keys. They were shaking. "Why?" she repeated.

Then she stood and stretched. Stretching felt good after so long sitting in the same position at the piano. Playing had helped her process all the stunning things she'd learned this afternoon.

But it hadn't stopped her from feeling torn in two. She'd loved Maman and Maman had loved her. But now she had to face a sobering truth. Maman had cared for her, loved her and protected her, yes. But every word out of her mouth had been a lie. And she'd kept Rose with her, not for Rose's sake, but for her own.

Sighing, she got up from the piano and walked downstairs to check that the door was locked. When she flipped the light off, she saw a movement in the shadows on the other side of the street, where a duplex that had been damaged in Katrina stood dark and empty.

It loomed like a defiant reminder of the massively destructive hurricane. Its windowpanes glinted jagged as shark's teeth in the pale glow from the few streetlights that hadn't been broken by vandals with air rifles or slingshots.

Rose froze, narrowing her gaze to a squint and holding her breath, waiting to see if whatever had moved was still there.

This was all she needed, after this afternoon. She curled her fingers, imagining how satisfying it would feel to wrap them around Detective Dixon Lloyd's neck and squeeze. It was his fault she was jumping at shadows.

A flicker of something drew her attention back to the abandoned house. She squinted. Out of the dimness shone a faint red glow, like the end of a cigarette. Was there someone smoking inside the abandoned house?

The red glow moved back and forth, back and forth, passing the jagged windows like the single red eye of a big cat that paced restlessly in its cage.

She kept losing sight of the red dot, then finding it again. She rubbed her eyes. Maybe if she opened the door she could see better. The beveled diamond-shaped insert in the door with its clear-and-red alternating panes distorted everything.

She looked behind her. All the lights on the ground floor were out, so whoever was over there shouldn't be able to see her. Easing the door open, she caught sight of the red glow again, and again it disappeared. At that very instant, she felt a whisper of *something* across her skin—a breeze? Or her imagination?

Goose bumps pebbled the flesh of her arms and she heard Maman's voice in her ear. *A goose walked over your grave. That's why they call them goose bumps.*

She crossed her arms and hugged herself, but she didn't close the door. She'd told Dixon she wasn't afraid. Now she knew that she'd lied. She *was,* but she'd be damned if a vagrant taking shelter in an abandoned building or a kid sneaking around looking for trouble would cause her to cower in her house.

She lifted her chin and stared defiantly at the point in the middle of a broken window where she'd last seen the red glow. As she did a bright light flared—like a match.

A thrill of caution rippled through her, but she tamped it down as much as she could. The vagrant—or the kid—was lighting another cigarette. That was all.

Staring at the flickering match flame, she waited to see the red flare that would signal the lighting of another cigarette, but it didn't come.

Instead, the match's light climbed higher, until it glowed on a dark seamed face and reflected in glittering scarlet eyes that stared back at her like the eyes of a demon. They blinked slowly, then widened, and she could see white all around the red, blazing pupils.

While she watched, mesmerized, her hand to her throat, the flame went out. The window was dark again. It was as if nothing had been there at all.

She forced her hand to relax, then went inside and pushed the door closed.

Or tried to.

It caught on something.

Rose started, looked down and gasped. A large foot in a leather shoe blocked the door.

Rose reacted instinctively, pushing at the door with all her might. Her scalp burned with panic. She sucked in a breath, preparing to scream.

"Hey, Rose."

Dixon. Her breath whooshed out and her arms and legs turned to jelly. As he pushed the door open she struggled to suck in air past her constricted throat.

"Wha—what are you doing?" she finally managed to croak.

"I saw you at the door. I was coming to see you."

She threw her head back and rolled her eyes. "You scared me! You could have let me know you were out there."

"Hey, I just walked up." He frowned at her. "What's the matter?"

"Nothing," she said quickly, noticing her hand was still at her throat. She relaxed it and let it fall to her side. "I was thinking about how early it's getting dark." She frowned at him. "What are you doing here?"

"I came to check on you." He stood at the door and looked out. "You were looking at something. What was it?"

"I told you, nothing," she said quickly—too quickly.

"You were looking at that empty building, weren't you? Is that what spooked you?"

Damn him. It seemed as if he could read her mind. Although more likely, he'd seen the direction she was looking when he walked up.

"No," she said weakly. Then more firmly, "No. *You* spooked me."

He turned and looked at her. "What did you see?"

She gave an exasperated sigh, then spread her

hands. "Okay. Fine. It was just a light, like a cigarette. Kind of a red glow. But then it went out and he—whoever—lit a match." She shuddered.

"Then what? Tell me why it upset you." Dixon stepped beside her and placed his hand on the small of her back. She felt the warmth seep into her skin through the finely woven cotton blouse. She closed her eyes and wished she could melt into his touch. The slight pressure of his hand on her back felt comforting and protective. But it also stirred something inside her. Something she hadn't felt since—ever.

Or at least since she could remember. Her insides thrilled and fluttered at his touch.

"Rose?"

"It upset me because you've got me jumping at cobblywobbles."

"Cobbly what?"

She waved a hand. "It's just a word Maman used. A word for things that aren't there."

But despite her brave words, she couldn't take her eyes off the dark building, afraid that any second, she'd see those awful eyes again.

"The match flared and lit up a face." Her hand doubled into a fist at her chest. "It was awful, like a devil's mask, with red eyes."

She waited for him to laugh, to tell her she was right about the cobblywobbles. In fact, she wished he would, even though she knew it wasn't true.

Maybe if Dixon said it aloud, his confidence, his assurance would change ominous reality into silly fantasy.

But he didn't laugh or protest what she'd said. Instead, he studied the building. "I think I'll go check it out. I've got a high-powered flashlight in my car."

"You're going to go in there?"

"Yeah. I want to see if anyone's there, or has been there recently." He looked at her. "And when I get back, I want you to be packed and ready to go with me. You're staying at my place until I figure out who's after you."

She clenched her fist even tighter, as if she were holding on to the last shred of control she had over her life. She didn't want to give in to the fear that lurked in a dark corner of her heart. The fear that caused the nightmares, that caused the migraines. The fear of whoever had cut her and left her for dead.

"No. I've got piano students. I've got… This is my home. I'm safe here."

Dixon blew out a frustrated breath between his teeth. "We'll talk about this when I get back. For now, lock and dead bolt the door. I'll knock like this." He gave a brisk, unique knock—one, then two quick raps, then two more. "You'll know it's me."

Rose watched him pull his weapon from the paddle holster at the small of his back and check it.

"Oh, are you going to use that?" she gasped.

"Yes," Dixon said wryly. "It's why I have it."

"That's so dangerous. What if he has a gun, too? He could kill you. What if you don't—"

"Come back?" His mouth quirked. "Rose, you can count on me. I'll always come back." He stepped outside. "Lock the door."

She closed the door and locked the dead bolt. The light from the streetlamps cast his tall shadow on the glass of the door. It reminded her of the first time he'd come to see her. As she watched, his shadow moved away and blended into all the other shadows along the street.

With her heart in her throat, Rose turned off the landing light and sat down on the fifth step, feeling in the pocket of her skirt for her cell phone. If it looked like Dixon was in trouble, she'd call 911.

She sat there for fifteen minutes, timed on her phone, and didn't see a thing. No creeping shadows, no glowing cigarette. Not even Dixon's flashlight.

When his shadow darkened the door, she jumped. He rapped on the glass. She was up and undoing the dead bolt before he finished the unique knock he'd promised to use.

He came in and closed the door. "Get your stuff. You're going with me."

Rose shook her head. "I told you, no. I'm not going to let some vagrant or—or doped-up kid run me out of my home." She gestured toward the empty house. "I didn't see a thing. Did you go inside?"

He nodded. "Let's go upstairs," he said, glancing behind him. He started up without waiting for her to answer.

She followed him into the kitchen. "You think he's still out there?"

"I don't know," he said. "I don't want to take the chance, though."

"What did you do? I never saw your flashlight."

"That's because the windows of that building are boarded up, tightly. All of them."

"Boarded?" She remembered then that the windows did have plywood over them. "But—I saw that light. That match."

"Whoever it was must have been standing on the street in front of the building."

"But I didn't see anything except the upper part of his face. His eyes. It was like a grotesque mask, floating in the…" She stopped when his sharp eyes snapped to hers. She folded her arms and gave a tiny shrug.

He held out his hand. He was holding a matchbook by its edges between his fingers. "This matchbook was on the sidewalk in front of the building."

She looked at it. The front said *Doll's Diner, Angola, Louisiana.* "He dropped it?"

"Don't know. Maybe he left it on purpose."

"I don't understand."

Dixon took a handkerchief from his pocket and wrapped the matchbook in it, then pocketed it. "Angola is where the state penitentiary is."

"What does that mean?" she asked.

He shook his head. "Maybe nothing. It's just a hunch. I'm going to have the matchbook checked for prints, but I'm pretty sure there won't be any. The important thing is that you weren't imagining things. There was definitely somebody out there."

She wrapped her arms around herself. "He did it on purpose."

"Did what?"

"Lit that match and held it up to his face. He was trying to scare me."

Dixon's left brow went up. "You saw his eyes. Did you recognize him?"

"No." She heard the hesitation in her voice. She hadn't recognized him. But should she have?

Suddenly, fed by that question, floodgates opened in her mind and all the questions she had never asked herself—never dared to—came gushing forward to the front of her consciousness.

Should she have recognized the man who'd stood there in the dark and stared at her over the red-gold light of a match? Had he been the man who had attacked her with a knife, scarred her and left her for dead?

Dixon watched Rose's expression morph from thoughtful to worried to terrified. He wanted to ask her if she'd remembered something, but somehow, he knew that would be a mistake. So he settled for touching her arm and asking, "Rose? What is it?"

She gave a little start. "Oh, nothing." She smoothed the tiny wrinkles between her brows with her fingertips. "I was just wondering if I should have recognized him." Her gaze flitted toward the empty building across the street, then back to Dixon. "But I didn't."

"Well, you won't have to worry about him anymore because you're going with me," he said firmly. "Now pack a bag."

Her chin lifted and her eyes turned cold as amber. "How many times do I have to tell you I am not leaving this house. It's my home. The only home I've ever—ever known." Her gaze took the temperature from cold to freezing. "Besides, I have obligations. Piano students who depend on my being here."

He almost retorted that she could be putting her students in danger by continuing her lessons, but he bit his lip. Was that going too far? Would whoever was following her stoop to frightening or harming children? Because Dixon wasn't acting in an official capacity, working on an NOPD open case, he couldn't force her to go with him.

So there was only one way to make sure she and her students were safe.

He shrugged and gave her a crooked smile. "Then I'll stay here."

Chapter Eight

"Stay here? No! That's impossible. You can't." Rose stammered.

Dixon held up the gym bag he'd fetched from his car. "I figured you wouldn't leave. So I planned ahead. I packed a toothbrush and everything," he said congenially. "Now, where can I sleep?"

Rose opened her mouth, then closed it again. She gazed at him narrowly. For a moment he thought she might tell him to leave, or at the very least to sleep on the floor by the front door.

But then she turned on her heel and walked through the kitchen door into the hall. Instead of continuing straight across into the living room, she turned to the right and walked down a narrow hallway.

"This is where I sleep," she said, indicating the first door on the left. "You can sleep in there." She nodded at a second door. "This first door on the right is the bathroom. That last door is a storage closet."

Rose opened the door she'd indicated as his and flipped on the light. Then she gasped.

Dixon went on full alert, his hand going for his weapon before he saw what she'd seen. On the four-poster bed, draped over the white quilted spread, was a pile of what looked to him like terry cloth. It was stained. Dark streaks and spatters covered it.

He stepped past Rose and walked over to the bed and picked it up. It was a bathrobe. His fists clenched around the material.

It was the robe that had been missing from Rosemary Delancey's apartment. The robe that matched the sash tied to the bedposts on the blood-covered bed.

He turned to find her staring at it. She looked as though she were looking at a ghost. Had someone been in her house? Had someone sneaked in and left this?

"Rose, did you know this was here?" he asked, searching her face.

She blinked, then tore her gaze away from the bloodstained robe and looked at him. "Yes," she said quietly. "I found it this afternoon and put it in here. I didn't...think I'd see it again so...so soon."

"Where was it?"

"In Maman's closet."

Dixon's pulse pounded. "Was there anything else? Anything that could identify you?"

She shook her head. "Just…" She gestured toward the robe.

"I need to take this. It's evidence," Dixon said. "When we find out who hurt you, this will help convict him."

Rose nodded again. "Please," she said. "Just get it out of here."

He nodded. Looking around, he noticed the white box. He quickly folded the robe and stowed it in the box. "I'll take it in with me in the morning. Tonight it can stay in here with me."

She didn't say anything; she just looked at him.

"Was this Maman Renée's room?" he asked.

Rose shook her head. "No, it was mine. I moved into Maman's room after…" Her voice broke.

Dixon squeezed her shoulder. Her head turned slightly toward him but she didn't recoil from his touch.

"I know it's hard," he said gently. "Five months isn't a long time. You can't believe it now, but it will get better."

"You sound like you know." She peered up at him.

He let go of her shoulder and leaned against the door facing. "I do. My parents were killed in a car wreck when I was fifteen and Dee was nine."

"Oh, Dixon, I'm so sorry," Rose said. "Dee is your sister?"

He nodded. "Delilah."

"And she was only nine? Were you put in foster care?"

Dixon smiled wryly. "Nope. We lived in the Ninth Ward. It was a lot like this neighborhood, actually. The people in the area took care of us."

"But what about your aunts? Or uncles?"

He shook his head. "Just me. I dropped out of school and got a job."

"Oh, Dixon."

He shrugged. "We did okay," he said. "I just wanted you to know that you won't always feel like this."

Rose rubbed her temple. "I know that—I mean, I guess I do. But it's not just that I miss her. I do. But I found out some things today."

"Things?"

"Bing told me that Maman knew the whole time who I was. She hid me away on purpose." She took in a shaky breath. "She'd had a daughter who'd died. I was just her daughter's replacement." Her voice rose in pitch.

"Rose, I know how hard this must be—"

"You know. You *know!*" she cried, clenching her fists at her side. "You think you know so much, but you don't know anything. You barge into my life like a—a football tackle or something. You've got your eyes on the ball and so you just mow down everybody and everything in your way—" she took a sharp, stuttering breath

"—because all that matters to you is results. You don't care who you hurt." She stopped suddenly and hiccuped.

For an instant, Dixon thought she might burst into hysterical tears. Her eyes were wet and beginning to turn red. But she lifted her chin and glared at him.

"Just like this," she went on. "You show up at my door, not to see how I'm doing, not to ask what you can do for me. No. You show up here and bully your way inside because that's what *you* think I need." She thumped his chest with her index finger.

He put his hands on her shoulders, as gently as before. She stiffened, but not for one second did her gaze waver. A single glistening tear spilled over from one eye and made its way slowly down her cheek.

"I'm sorry, Rose. I hate that you feel that way about me."

"But not enough to change your mind. You're still going to insist on staying here, aren't you? Whether I want you to or not."

"Yes, I am." He let go of her shoulders. He needed to step back, to put some space between them. "I can't stand the idea that something might happen and I wouldn't be here."

Acting on a stupid urge, he brushed his thumb across her chin. "Listen to me. No matter what you think, no matter what it looks like, I am here because you're in danger. Real danger."

Then he really did have to put some distance between them. He walked over to the window that faced Prytania Street and parted the curtains just enough to peer out.

"You were right the other day about being afraid I'd brought the danger to you." He turned and looked at her. "But the truth is, the only reason I found you was because someone saw you and recognized you."

Rose folded her arms protectively at her waist. Dixon saw her shoulders stiffen and her face crumple.

"Someone saw me? Recognized me? Who?"

"Nobody. A two-bit thug. The important thing is I'm here."

Rose shook her head. "Maybe to you that's what's important." She wrung her hands.

"Oh, I don't know if I can take this much longer. Everything Maman told me, everything she did to keep me safe was a lie." She shook her head as if trying to dislodge her thoughts. Her eyes grew damp again.

"For twelve years she hid me from the world and made sure the truth never made it past the front door."

"Rose, hey," Dixon said, reaching for her. "I'm sure Maman did what she thought was best."

"Are you? You think she didn't know what she was doing? Of course she did."

"I don't deny that she was wrong to keep you hidden—"

"Don't you get it? My Maman, the one person in the world I trusted, looked me in the eye every day and lied to me. *Every day.* She read the papers, saw all the news stories about Rosemary Delancey. She knew who I was and never told me." Rose put her hands over her mouth.

"Oh…" she moaned, her voice muffled. "How could she do that? How could she have kept me here like—like Rapunzel, trapped in her tower? Do you know we never talked about that night? I was afraid to ask and she never—all she ever said was, *You're safe now. Maman will keep you safe.* And all the time, she had that robe—that proof, locked away in the closet."

Then she broke down and cried.

Without thinking it through, Dixon pulled Rose into his arms. She came easily, flattening her palms against his chest and burying her face in the curve between his shoulder and neck. Her tears wet his skin. He buried his nose in her hair and drew in the scent of honeysuckle that always surrounded her.

He cupped the back of her head in his palm and felt her relax as he gently massaged her nape.

Rocking slightly, he didn't speak, just held her as her sobs slowly faded to an occasional sniffle.

He had no idea how long he stood there like that, holding her, torturing himself. He grew hard, but he set his jaw and ignored it. This wasn't about his needs.

With a small sigh, she moved closer, melting against him. Too close. He stepped backward a half step, even though it was too late. He felt his face heat in embarrassment.

Rose's gaze met his. Her eyes were wide and her cheeks flushed. Her lips were slightly parted. As he watched, her tongue flicked out to moisten them. He grew harder.

"Rose?" he whispered, mesmerized by her dewy eyes.

She didn't say anything, but she didn't move, either.

Knowing he was making a fatal mistake but unable to stop himself, he bent his head and touched her lips with his. The brief soft feel of skin against skin heated his blood.

Rose gasped quietly. Gasped, but didn't recoil. The air she drew in cooled his lower lip and stoked the flames of desire rising inside him.

Then she lifted her head—*lifted* it without his urging—and pressed her mouth to his. Her eyes drifted shut as he pulled her to him and kissed her, still tentative, still waiting for her to back away or push at him or something.

"Dixon?" she whispered.

He froze. Was it a sigh or a question? He lifted his head and looked into her eyes. "Are you okay?" he asked.

She stared at him unblinkingly. "I don't know."

"I'm sorry," he said, stepping backward. "I shouldn't have—"

She touched his mouth with her fingertips. "Shh. Don't. I've read books, watched movies, but I've never—I don't remember ever being held, being kissed." Tears welled in her eyes. "How can I not remember anything?"

"I don't know." His erection throbbed. The thought that he'd been the first man in her memory to touch her lips with his was so erotic and at the same time so humbling.

He touched her shoulder and she stepped into his arms again. He nuzzled her silky, sweet-smelling hair. "The theory of amnesia is that you're blocking out memories that are too painful or too awful to deal with. It's called dissociative amnesia. It's generally caused by a traumatic event."

Rose's hand touched the scar at her hairline. "How do you know all that?" she asked.

"I talked to the department shrink about it a little. He said that—"

She went rigid and her head shot up. "You talked to a psychiatrist about me?"

"Not about you specifically."

She uttered a short, sharp laugh and pulled away from him.

If her glare were a laser, he'd be sliced neatly in half.

"Not about me *specifically,*" she said archly. "What does that mean?"

Dixon frowned. "I was very careful not to use any names or dates. All I did was ask him how someone could lose all memory of their life before a certain moment and he said that usually dissociative amnesia is caused by an injury or a traumatic event, like your attack."

"And what else did you tell him? I can't believe he let your questions go without asking you who you were talking about." She took another step backward, away from him.

He nodded. "He did. He asked me if I was working on an amnesia case, but I didn't tell him anything. I just said I'd always thought people who claimed to have amnesia were faking."

"Faking," Rose echoed.

"I don't anymore," he said quickly. Somehow he suddenly felt as if he'd stepped into quicksand. He was sinking fast. "He explained that it's a real condition."

Rose's back was stiff, her chin was lifted and

her eyes were still as hot and cutting as amber lasers. "Well, thank goodness he explained it to you. I'm so grateful that you no longer think I'm a *liar*."

"Come on, Rose, that's not what I meant."

"Isn't it?" Her hand went to her temple. He wasn't sure if she was touching the scar or massaging a headache. What he did know was that he'd hurt her and made her angry. He wasn't exactly sure why. All he'd done was seek out an explanation for her inability to remember anything about her life before she'd been attacked.

"Rose, I'm sorry. I didn't mean to upset you."

But he could see that his apology was too little too late. "I promise you I'm going to find out who did this to you and I'm going to make sure he pays. In the meantime, I'm going to stay here. I'm not going to let anything happen to you."

Rose didn't respond. She swept past him like a queen. He turned to watch her as she walked regally to the door to her bedroom and went inside, slamming it behind her.

MONDAY MORNING DIXON was at his desk early. On his way in to work he had checked in with Ray, who told him, just as he had on Sunday morning, that he hadn't seen anybody around the shop. Not Saturday night and not Sunday night.

Dixon had thanked him and asked him to keep up the drive-bys for another couple of days.

He sighed as he counted the stack of reports he needed to review. He wanted to get through them and get them off his desk before noon so he could head up to Angola to talk to T-Bo Pereau. That meant he had to complete one every half hour.

But first, he reached into his file drawer and pulled out the file on the case the newspapers at the time had dubbed The Beauty Queen Murder. He knew everything in the file by heart, but he wanted to read over a couple of things, just to refresh his memory.

He searched through the typewritten pages until he found the statement made by Lyndon Banker's father. Dixon hadn't forgotten how guilty and grief-stricken the man had been when he'd interviewed him. Eldridge Banker had told Dixon and his partner that he'd thrown Lyndon out of the house the week before.

I was just trying to teach him a lesson, Dixon read from the transcription of the interview. *He'd gone through all the money my wife's mother had left him, and before I realized it and cut him off, he was depleting my accounts and was in hock to a loan shark. Gambling.*

This was what Dixon had been looking for. He read through the rest of Banker's statement but didn't find any mention of the loan shark's name.

"Damn it," he muttered. He turned pages until he came to the report written by Detective James

Shively, who'd been his partner when he first joined the homicide division. He quickly skimmed it.

There. He tapped the page. Shively had figured the loan shark Banker had mentioned in his statement was a Gretna, Louisiana, businessman named George Innes. At the time, Innes seemed to have a monopoly on drugs and money around the Touro Bouligny and Irish Channel areas of the city. Shively's report mentioned that there were a couple of youngsters who were trying to get a foot in the door, seeing as Innes was about to turn eighty.

Shively's theory was that Rosemary's fiancé had gotten caught in the crossfire of a turf war.

Dixon sighed and put away the file. He had to get started on those reports if he wanted to get up to Angola today. He made a mental note to check with Shively, who was now retired, about the up-and-coming young loan sharks he'd referred to in his report. Then he'd call Vice and find out who was in charge of loan-sharking these days.

It was after ten before Ethan came in carrying two cups of coffee. Dixon was deep into his fourth report.

"How'd the moving go?" Ethan asked.

"Movie?" Dixon popped the lid on the plastic cup and sipped carefully. It was hot and not too bad.

"Mov-*ing*. Your sister?" Ethan prompted. "The

reason you couldn't go to the scrimmage Saturday? Which was a great one, by the way. We got to spend some time with Brees."

"Yeah," Dixon said, signing off on the report in front of him and picking up another folder. "I hated to miss it."

"And after the bomb scare, we all went out for wings and beer."

"Sounds like you had a good time." Dixon sighed as the hot coffee slip down his throat. He could almost feel the caffeine beginning to work.

"Bull. You're not paying the least bit of attention to anything I've said," Ethan groused. "And I don't appreciate your lying to me, either."

Dixon looked up at his partner. "What's wrong with you this morning? What are you talking about?"

"There," Ethan said, spreading his arms in a what-are-you-going-to-do gesture. "I knew you weren't paying attention."

Dixon frowned as he replayed Ethan's remarks. "Did you say something about a bomb?"

Ethan laughed. "Good morning, Dix," he said wryly, sketching a little bow. "So what were you really doing on Saturday?"

Dixon groaned inwardly as he shrugged. "It was one of those days. Dee called me and told me I didn't have to help her." He didn't like lying to his partner, but he'd started this by claiming his sister needed his help. "So I just kind of goofed off," he finished lamely.

"In Jackson Square?"

Dixon's head snapped up. "What?" He felt his ears burning. Damn, he hoped he wasn't turning red.

"Jerreau saw you. Said he hollered at you and waved, but you were sitting on a bench staring into space."

Dixon shrugged. "Like I said, goofing around."

"You could have called me. Come on to the game."

"I didn't want to hassle the crowd. I'd have been late."

Ethan frowned at him. "You knew we were going out after."

"Come on, Delancey. You know I'm not a big partier." His attention kept shifting back to the report in front of him.

"Right. I sometimes forget how old you really are."

Dixon told Ethan what he thought about that remark.

"So what are you up to this morning?" Ethan asked, settling down at his desk.

"As soon as I clear out these reports, I'm headed up to Angola. I want to talk to Pereau some more."

"Pereau? You mean the skunk who said he'd seen Rosemary?"

Dixon nodded. "I want to see what else he knows. Who he talked to about her."

"You know you're around the bend, right? My cousin has been missing for twelve years. Whoever killed her probably dumped her in the river. The Mississippi rarely gives back."

"You're not the least bit interested in finding out why a two-bit druggie like Pereau would claim to have seen her? He could have tried to sell you the information, once he found out who you were, but he didn't."

"No, because he had enough sense to see that you were the softer touch. I'm telling you, Dix, you're wasting your time. Any skell off the street hears the name Delancey and there they go. Spinning tales of what *really* happened. It gets boring after a while."

"Then I'll be bored."

Ethan stared at Dixon pensively. "Why're you doing this?"

Dixon leaned back in his chair and stretched and yawned. "Damn, I hate doing reports. Makes my neck stiff." Then he sat back up. "I've always wanted to close that case. It was my first as a homicide detective. From what I saw, the killer didn't have time to kill the fiancé and get back to Rosemary's apartment and disappear with her."

"Right. You think she…" Ethan shook his head and huffed.

"I think she walked out on her own. I think she survived."

"You don't have one shred of evidence. And I swear, Dix, if you start digging into this and upset my family, you'll be up to your butt in alligators. Got it?"

"Don't worry. This is just me. I'm not telling anybody. And I promise you, if this trip leads to nothing, I'll let it go." Dixon felt confident in his promise. He was convinced that Pereau knew more than he'd told them, and he planned to squeeze every last drop of information out of the punk.

Chapter Nine

It took Dixon over two hours to drive up to Angola. On the way, he'd called Shively, hoping he still had the same number. He hadn't talked to his old partner in several months.

After exchanging pleasantries, Dixon told Shively why he'd called. "You said something in your report about a couple of kids nipping at Innes's heels."

"Yeah," Shively said. "There was always a lot of controversy about Innes—where he got all the money he seemed to have access to. Folks had basically two theories."

Dixon could picture his partner counting off on his fingers. "One, Innes was a front for some truly wealthy SOB who didn't want to get his hands dirty but liked the return on investment, or two, the money was coming from out of town. Some people thought it might be Tito Vega, who operated on the Mississippi Gulf Coast, but nobody was ever able to pin him down."

"But Innes was pushing eighty back then. Who took over?"

"I don't know. There were a couple of guys nipping at Innes's heels. Seems like I heard they agreed to divide up the territory." Shively paused. "I've got a buddy on the Gretna police force you could call. But seems like an import from up north named Wasabe was bidding on Touro Bouligny and the Channel."

"Wasabe?"

"Yeah. I forget his first name. Allen or Aaron or something like that. I think he owns an accounting firm somewhere on Tchoupitoulas. So," Shively said, "what's got you dredging up ancient history?"

Dixon explained as much as he could without giving Shively any specifics.

"You know, it's odd," Shively said. "That case was your first homicide, and it was nearly my last."

Dixon knew exactly what Shively was talking about. A few months later, as he and Shively were working a faked suicide, Shively was shot. After he recovered, he sat at a desk for about a year, then retired.

"For some reason," Shively went on, "it stuck with me. All that blood on the floors, the bed, the bathtub."

"Yeah," Dixon said, his mouth twisting wryly. "It stuck with me, too."

After another minute or so of catching up, Dixon thanked Shively and hung up, promising to get by to see him and have a beer soon. It was after two by the time he found himself waiting at one of the tiny scarred tables in the visitation room.

When the guard brought T-Bo Pereau in, and he spotted Dixon, the wiry Cajun's swarthy face turned a sickly green. He balked, but the guard half dragged him over and pushed him down in the chair.

Dixon met the guard's eyes and angled his head dismissively, then turned to T-Bo. "Afternoon," he said cheerily.

T-Bo was half-turned in his chair, not looking at Dixon. He tried to speak without moving his thin, pinched lips. "What you call me out here for, eh? Folks see me talking wit' you, I'll be dead for sure."

"Then you might want to hurry up and tell me what I need to know."

"I told you everything already. Dat's all I know." T-Bo's color was returning a little, but sweat rolled down his face, despite the air-conditioned room. He sent a narrow sidelong gaze toward the cardboard package Dixon carried.

"That whole carton for me?" he asked.

"Hit and run. DWI. His papa wouldn't bail him out. Said he needed to learn a lesson."

Dixon shifted. That information sounded familiar. "I still haven't heard a name. Who's your friend, T-Bo? I'm about to start thanking you for all your great information, and I won't be whispering."

T-Bo leaned back and crossed his arms again. He sent a guarded glance around the room. "Cigarettes," he said.

Dixon pushed the carton across the little table.

"Junior Fulbright," T-Bo mouthed. "Now get outta here."

It took Dixon a second to process the name. "The councilman's son?" he asked.

T-Bo shrugged. "I reckon."

James Fulbright was a city councilman known to be hard on crime. So hard that he'd let his son serve time for a DUI. Again, Dixon felt a chill. T-Bo's information was too on-target. He *was* telling the truth.

"Who all did you tell about her?"

T-Bo's eyes went dull. "Nobody."

"You're a lying snake," Dixon said. "Stand up. I need to give you that hug for all the great information you've given me."

"There might have been a couple people standing around when Junior was talking."

Dixon shifted. "I swear on my mama's grave—"

"Okay! Sure!" T-Bo hissed. "I swear I don't know who all was around, but Junior wasn't quiet about it. He was high and dying to brag. Said he might try to sell the info. Said whoever tried to kill her back then would want to know where she was."

"Where'd this conversation take place?"

"Down on Bourbon, corner of Rampart. And that's all I know." He shoved his chair back violently and grabbed the cigarettes. "I told you to leave me the hell alone. You *couyon*. I ain't talking to the likes of you."

Dixon rose and frowned menacingly. "Give me back those smokes, then."

"Hell no. You gave 'em to me, fair and square."

A guard started their way, but Dixon waved him off with a brief shake of his head. He wanted to make this good, for T-Bo's sake.

"Fine, T-Bo. Enjoy them," he said, nodding at the carton. "Because it's the last you'll get." At that he turned on his heel and gestured to the guard. "Take me to the warden. I need to talk to him about revoking some privileges."

AFTER THE TWO-HOUR drive back to the precinct, Dixon found a sheet of paper on his desk. It was the fingerprint report from the cigarette lighter the punk dropped the other day when Dixon chased him. The prints belonged to a James Fulbright Jr. Dixon whistled softly.

Then he touched his mouse and entered James Fulbright Jr.'s name into the system. When the profile page came up and Dixon saw the photo, Dixon whistled again. "I will be damned," he whispered. "Hello, Ponytail."

The photo was of a young man, early twenties, with spiked dirty blond hair. He was definitely the punk who had followed Rose on the streetcar, and the fingerprints on the cigarette lighter confirmed it.

So Junior was gathering information about Rose, which he planned to turn around and sell to whoever showed the most interest. Dixon turned his attention to Junior's rap sheet. Skimming it quickly, he saw several DUIs, a couple of disorderly conducts and even one resisting arrest.

He thought about Junior's dad. City councilman James Fulbright was known to be hard on crime. So when Junior finally hit somebody while driving drunk, Daddy Fulbright let him go to the slammer. A cold move, given the state of the prisons in Louisiana.

Dixon searched online until he came up with a photo of Rosemary with James Fulbright all dressed up with crowns and robes during Mardi Gras, 1999. He remembered talking to Fulbright back then. The councilman had praised Rosemary, saying she was a sweet girl and he couldn't imagine why anyone would want to harm her.

Dixon looked at the councilman's face. Just how far would he go to further his fight against crime in the city? He'd let his own teenaged son spend time in prison. Could he have targeted Lyndon Banker, hurting Rosemary because she was in his way? It was something to think about.

But right now, he needed information on Junior's whereabouts. He wanted to speed over to the Fulbrights' home and demand the information, but that probably wouldn't be a good idea, especially if he used his official capacity to get the information. No, when he talked to Councilman Fulbright, he'd do it on his own time, and he wouldn't mention Rosemary Delancey.

He printed a copy of Junior's photo. Just as he grabbed it off the printer, Ethan came in.

"You missed a good one," Ethan said.

"Yeah?" he responded as he folded up the sheet of paper and stuck it in his jacket pocket.

"We had a jumper on the Riverwalk."

Dixon looked up. "A jumper. No kidding?"

"Yeah. For a while I wasn't sure we could stop her. She was young—early twenties at the outside. Apparently she found out her parents paid off her boyfriend to leave her alone—and he took the money."

"How'd you talk her down?"

Ethan flopped down in his desk chair and stretched. "I'll tell you how. Because you left me here on my own, when the call came in, the lieutenant paired me with Burgess."

Dixon didn't speak, just nodded, biting the inside of his cheek to keep from laughing. Mary Burgess was a ten-year veteran known for being tough on crime, tougher on her partner and toughest on herself.

"How did that go?" Dixon asked.

"Good. Really good. Surprised the hell out of me. She talked the girl down. She was...sweet."

"Burgess? Sweet?"

"Yeah. Go figure," Ethan said. "So what did you find out on your fishing expedition to Angola?"

Dixon handed Ethan the photo of Junior Fulbright he'd just taken off the printer.

"Who's this?" Ethan asked, although the photo was footnoted with name and date of birth.

"Junior Fulbright."

"The city councilman's son." It wasn't a question. "Not surprised. He can't stay out of trouble to save his life." Ethan handed the picture back to him. "What's Junior got to do with your BFF Pereau?"

"He's the punk—" Dixon almost said *who was following Rose.* He stopped himself just in time. He wasn't ready to tell Ethan that he'd found his cousin. "—who told Pereau about spotting your cousin. If he'd really told him. Hard to believe that even on the street, Junior Fulbright would be hanging with the likes of T-Bo. My bet is that T-Bo overheard Junior talking to someone else."

Ethan shot him a disgusted look. "What did Pereau tell you Junior said?"

"Said Junior claimed he knew her from Mardi Gras the year she was queen of Carnival."

Ethan tossed the photo back to Dixon. "Right. What is he? Twenty-something? Like he'd recognize Rosemary even if he did see her, which, may I remind you, is a crock."

Dixon picked up the photo where it had fluttered to the floor. "Yeah, well. T-Bo isn't super-reliable."

"So it was a dead end after all? See, Dix? What did I tell you? There's always a story about a Delancey floating around out there."

Dixon didn't even try to argue. He didn't want to get into whether Rosemary was really alive with Ethan again. His partner was not a bit happy that Dixon had pursued T-Bo's remark this long. He put the mug shot in a binder and set it on the edge of his desk to take home with him. "Yeah," he said grudgingly, "I see what you mean."

He hated lying to his partner, even by omission, but both Rose and Ethan, as well as the rest of their family, deserved answers, and all he had right now were questions.

THAT EVENING AFTER he got off work, Dixon drove to the Fulbrights' home in Metairie, the only address he had for Junior. When he knocked on the door, the councilman answered.

"Councilman Fulbright, I'm Dixon Lloyd. I'm a detective with NOPD. We've met before, twelve years ago, when I was investigating the murder of Rosemary Delancey."

Fulbright nodded, frowning. "Yes?"

"I wonder if I could ask you a few questions about your son?"

Fulbright went pale. "Is he all right?"

Dixon held up his hands. "He's fine as far as I know, sir. I apologize for giving you a scare. My questions involve something he told another party regarding another case I'm working on."

Fulbright stepped backward to let Dixon inside. "Go right in there, to the left. That's my study."

Dixon waited for the councilman to sit in a leather club chair, then sat himself.

"I haven't seen my son in a couple of months," Fulbright said. "What is it you want to know?"

"Actually, I'd like to talk to him, so if you have any idea where he is, I'd appreciate the information."

The older man eyed Dixon with suspicion. "You're sure you're not looking for him in connection with a crime?"

"I have no knowledge of any illegal activities

on your son's part. It seems that he may have seen a missing person. I want to talk to him to find out if he has any information about that person's whereabouts."

"What missing person?"

"I'm afraid I can't answer that, sir. It's confidential."

Fulbright frowned. "I'm familiar with police tactics, Detective. I need your word that you're not going to arrest him."

Dixon nodded. "Unless he does something between now and the time I talk to him, I have no reason to do anything except ask him some questions," he said. "You do have my word."

Fulbright rubbed his chin as he studied Dixon. Finally, he sighed. "My son has been in some trouble in the past, but he tells me he's trying to straighten up. He enrolled in Delgado Community College. Last time I talked to him, he said he was looking to rent a house near the campus."

"Which campus? City Park?"

The councilman nodded.

"Does he have a cell phone?"

"It's on my plan." Fulbright gave Dixon his son's cell phone number.

Dixon thanked him for his cooperation. As he left, Fulbright stood at the front door and called out to him.

"Detective, if my son has broken the law, don't

give him special treatment. My stance on crime—
you know."

"Yes, sir," Dixon answered. He drove over to
the Delgado campus at City Park and checked
with the registrar's office. He didn't want to call
Junior and alert him that he was looking for him.
Sure enough James Fulbright Jr., was registered
for twelve hours of class work, enough to qualify
him as a full-time student.

After getting his address by flashing his badge,
Dixon drove to the Premier Apartments on General
Diaz Street and knocked on Unit 5.

When the door swung open and the bleary-eyed
punk who'd followed Rose on the streetcar focused
his squinty eyes on Dixon, he tried to shove
the door shut, but Dixon easily stopped it.

He held up his badge. "James Fulbright Jr.?"

"Whaddaya want?" the kid mumbled.

"I think you know what I want," Dixon said,
still blocking the door. "Aren't you going to invite
me in?"

"Whatever," Junior mumbled. He turned and
shuffled over to the couch and flopped down.

Dixon entered the dark, musty apartment and
closed the door behind him. The air was redolent
with marijuana smoke and mildew. The rickety,
scarred coffee table held an assortment of chip and
cookie bags, empty beer and soda cans and an ash-
tray full of pinched, hand-rolled butts, or roaches.

Dixon didn't miss the baggie Junior stuck behind the couch cushions as he lay down. "Come on, Junior. I didn't come here to bust you."

"Yeah?" he drawled. "Tell me another one."

"Sit up and concentrate," Dixon ordered him.

Junior just gave him a heavy-lidded stare, so Dixon walked over and with one sweeping gesture, pushed his dirty sneaker-clad feet off the couch.

"Hey!" Junior scrambled to a sitting position.

"Good. Now concentrate. I'll go slow for you. If you'll take a look at me I think you'll figure out why I'm here."

He sagged back against the couch cushions and closed his eyes.

Tired of the kid's rotten attitude, Dixon grabbed the neck of his ragged Saints sweatshirt and yanked him up until his face was within spitting distance.

"I said, look at me!"

"Okay, okay, geez!" Junior whined.

Dixon let go of his shirt.

Junior squinted. After a few seconds, his face became slightly more animated. "I know you," he said. "You're that hotshot who chased me all over town on Saturday."

"Right. *I* chased *you*. I think you've got it wrong. How about *you* followed a friend of mine."

"Huh?" Junior blinked, trying without success

to pull off an innocent expression. "I don't know what you're talking about."

"Listen to me, punk. Did you get a good look at this?" Dixon thrust his badge in front of Junior's eyes. "You know what it means? It means I can take you in and hold you for twenty-four hours for no reason at all. But…oh wait. Let me think a minute. I've *got* a reason, don't I? That baggie you hid. I'll bet it's got enough stuff in it to get you some time."

Junior's face drained of color. "Hey, you said you weren't going to bust me," he whined. "Please. My dad won't bail me out and I can't do time again."

The kid was really scared. "I said I didn't come here to bust you. I didn't say I wouldn't change my mind."

"Aw, man," the punk whined again. "What do you want? I'll tell you. Just don't arrest me."

"Then listen closely. I want to know who sicced you on the fortune-teller." He was careful not to give the slightest hint of Rose's name.

"The fortune-teller?" Junior was going bleary-eyed again, so Dixon grabbed his shirt.

"Stay with me, Junior. You think I missed the look you gave me as you swung up onto the street-car? You knew exactly what you were doing. Now, you tell me who paid you to follow her and I might forget that bag of weed. I'm sure it must have set you—or should I say, your daddy—back a couple of C-notes."

Suddenly, James Fulbright Jr. didn't look so good. His face turned pasty and sweat broke out on his forehead. "Nobody, I swear."

Dixon raised a brow. "*Nobody* can make you sweat in two seconds flat?"

"No," Junior said without conviction. His hand stole up to his temple to wipe away a drop of sweat.

"Come on, Junior. I know what you told T-Bo, and—"

"T-Bo ratted?" Junior spat out. "That stinking polecat. He's a dead man."

Dixon clucked. "Now, now, Junior. Are you threatening his life?"

Junior slumped. "No." He sniffled and wiped the back of his hand across his nose.

"That's good. You've got exactly three seconds to decide what you want to do. Get busted for possession or tell me who hired you to follow the fortune-teller?"

Junior shook his head in defeat. "I'm screwed. You take me in, I'll die in jail. If I rat, I'll be dead as T-Bo."

Dixon eyed the young punk. "What do you mean, 'dead as T-Bo'?" he asked. Had Junior heard somebody threatening the little Cajun?

"Yeah, yeah. I know he's not dead, yet. He ratted to a cop, though. He won't see another birth-day." Junior smiled. "Maybe not even another sunrise."

A cold chill slid down Dixon's spine. He'd call Angola just as soon as he finished here and tell the warden to put T-Bo in solitary. At that point, the little Cajun would definitely be exposed as a snitch, but at least he'd be alive.

"You better hope he sees a lot of sunrises and birthdays because otherwise, I'll make sure you get his old cell."

At those words Junior looked up, wide-eyed. "No, man," he whined. "I can't go back to prison."

"Totally up to you." Dixon watched him. The fear in his eyes turned to outright terror. Junior was more afraid of whoever had hired him than he was of prison.

Which was unfortunate for Dixon. He'd thought his best bet was to stick Junior behind bars and then bargain with him to get out. But in the last couple of minutes he'd decided that under the cir-cumstances, the last place he wanted Junior was in jail. He'd rather have him free, so he could follow him and find out where he went and who he met.

"Tell you what, punk. I'll just check back with you in a few days. How about that? Meanwhile, I'd suggest you quit lying around here and go to class, like you promised your daddy you would."

Junior sat up and narrowed his barely focused

eyes at him. "Yeah, sure. Okay. So you're not running me in?"

"Not today. But you think long and hard while I'm gone, and when I come back, you see if there isn't something you want to tell me. Got it?"

The kid was so relieved he looked like he might cry. "Yeah. Yes, sir. I got it. Yes, sir."

Dixon left the apartment and looked at his watch. He got into his car and drove a block away, then called Ethan's cousin Dawson Delancey. Dawson had a security agency, D&D Services. He just recently set up his new bride, Juliana, as his partner.

"Hey, Dawson, what's up?" he said when Dawson answered.

"Lloyd, you still babysitting my cousin?" Dawson replied.

"Ethan's coming along," Dixon said. "Doing pretty good."

"That's good to hear."

"Listen, Dawson, I've got a job for you, if you've got someone available. But I need him now."

"Grey Reed isn't on assignment. You mean literally now?"

Dixon didn't know Grey Reed, but he did know Dawson, and if Reed wasn't top-notch he wouldn't be working for him. "Yep, within the hour. I need him to follow Junior Fulbright around. I want to know who he talks to, who he goes to see…everything he does for the next couple of days."

"Junior Fulbright? The city councilman's son?"

"That's the one." Dixon gave him Junior's address.

"Reed will be there within a half hour."

Dixon thanked him, then hung up. He felt like he should stick around the punk's apartment until Reed got there, but he knew Dawson was as good as his word. Anyhow, he needed to go check on Rose.

Back in his car, he dialed Angola and got through to the warden. "I was afraid you'd be gone for the day," he said. "I wanted to talk to you about T-Bo Pereau—getting him into solitary, for his own safety."

"I'm afraid you're too late for that," the warden sighed. "I was just about to pick up the phone and call you."

"Why? What happened?" Dixon asked.

"Pereau was found in the showers, a bar of soap stuffed down his throat."

Chapter Ten

Dixon's stomach sank to his toes. Pereau was dead. "Did anyone see anything."

"No." The warden paused for a second, then said, "What the hell did you talk to him about?"

Dixon had anticipated that question, but he still grimaced as he dodged it. "I was just trying to confirm an ID. Who was in the showers with him?"

The warden gave a harsh laugh. "If I knew that, Lloyd, I wouldn't be in this job. I'd be a talk show psychic."

Anger and frustration sizzled through Dixon's veins. "When are you going to get some security cameras up there?"

The warden let go a few words that turned the air around Dixon's cell phone blue. He winced.

"I know, I know. So nobody saw nothing, right?"

"You got it."

"And you don't have any ideas?"

"I know who all I've got up here, and I know that a lot of them are connected, if you get my drift. But T-Bo ain't nothing but a two-bit drug dealer. It doesn't make sense."

"What doesn't?"

"The soap down the gullet? That's usually a message. *Keep your mouth shut.*"

"A message to whom? Once you've got a bar of soap down your throat you're not going to talk."

Another grating laugh crackled through the phone. "To his buddies, or to anybody else who thinks about ratting to a cop."

Dixon bristled, partly in indignation at the accusation, but also because he knew that he bore a lot of the responsibility for T-Bo's death. "T-Bo made it real clear that he wasn't talking to me."

"Don't play me for a fool, Lloyd. Your performance was hardly Oscar-worthy. You don't think the other inmates in the visitor room missed the fact that no matter what you said, T-Bo got his cigarettes?" The warden paused for a beat. "And I sure didn't forget that not three weeks ago, you called up here and asked for television privileges for him. If you know who did this, or why, you'd better tell me now."

"I wish I knew who. As far as why, T-Bo offered me some information having to do with an old case. But when I tracked it down, it was practically worthless." It wasn't exactly a lie, Dixon rationalized to himself. Yes, he'd found Rose-mary Delancey because of T-Bo, but he wasn't any closer to figuring out who had attacked her.

"That's why I came back to see him."

"And you gave him the cigarettes even though he refused to talk to you?"

"He didn't tell me anything that helped me on my case."

The warden spewed another mouthful of blue words. "If you're lying to me, Lloyd, you're an accessory."

"Give me a break," Dixon laughed. "You are doing an autopsy, aren't you?"

"S.O.P. And before you ask, yes, I'll give you the results. Although I don't think there's any doubt what killed him. I'll be in touch with you anyhow," the warden said. "I'm going to need a deposition about what you two talked about."

"No problem," Dixon said. "Let me know what the autopsy shows." He tossed the phone onto the passenger seat, then slammed the steering wheel with the heel of his hand. "Damn it!" he grated.

The danger was real. T-Bo's death confirmed it. Whoever had ordered T-Bo killed was the same person who'd tortured Rose. And Dixon knew without a doubt that he was coming to kill her.

SOMETHING WOKE DIXON. He was immediately aware that he wasn't in his bed at home. It took him no more than a fraction of a second to remember exactly where he was. He was in Rose's bed and she was on the other side of the wall.

He lay without moving, listening. Rain pelted the panes of the window beside his bed. He could see droplets crashing against the panes at an angle and running down in rivulets. Was that what had woken him?

No, he knew it wasn't. He'd heard something else. He pressed the lighted dial on his watch. It was a little after three in the morning. He pushed back the covers and pulled on his pants. He picked up his paddle holster and stuck it in his waistband and drew his weapon. It was probably nothing, but he hadn't been exaggerating when he'd told Rose that she was in danger.

Standing motionless, he listened. There. He heard it again. It was Rose. She was crying. He debated whether to check on her—for about two seconds. She was probably dreaming, but he wasn't taking any chances.

Opening the door to the hall, he saw the glow from a night-light shining through the open bathroom door.

He was at Rose's door in two steps. He stopped outside the door and listened again. He heard a strangled cry, then a wordless whimper. The muffled tone of her voice confirmed that she was in the throes of a bad dream. Again he debated.

Check on her or leave her to ride out her nightmare alone?

Then, through the door, he heard her gasp and cry.

"No, no," she moaned. "No—" The word was cut off by another gasp.

He quit questioning whether it was any of his business whether she slept well or badly. He was going in. He couldn't stand by and do nothing while she cried and gasped in fear—even if the fear wasn't grounded in reality.

Reaching out he grasped the glass doorknob and turned it slowly, carefully. It was almost noiseless. Then he eased the door open. The door slid smoothly and quietly on its hinges.

Rain was pounding against the windows of this room, too. Vague glows from the streetlamps cast eerie shadows on the walls. Shadows of translucent splashes and rivulets of droplets cascading downward like tears.

Rose was drawn up into fetal position under an intricately stitched, colorful quilt. Her black hair was splayed out across the pillow like ink swirling in water. She hadn't stirred when he'd slipped through the door. He could still hear her whimpering quietly. She seemed to be all right except for the dream that held her in thrall.

He stood there for a few seconds, watching her. She didn't move except for her lips as she murmured unintelligibly and her head, which rocked slightly back and forth as if she were trying to say no.

The urge to touch her, to smooth her wrinkled forehead and whisper in her ear that she was safe, that it was just a dream, overwhelmed him. But what if he woke her up? How terrifying would it be for her to be jolted out of her dream to find a man standing over her bed?

He didn't have to answer that question, though, because at that moment she jackknifed and went completely rigid. "No! No! No-o-o!" she panted. "Please! No!"

"Rose," Dixon whispered as he rushed to her side. She didn't wake up, but her brow furrowed, as if a part of her brain had heard him.

He brushed her temple with the backs of his curved fingers—no more than the brush of a butterfly's wing.

She winced. "No…" she muttered, then suddenly, her eyes popped open. They reflected the dim glow from the streetlamps. He could see that they were glazed with sleep and wet with tears as she met his gaze. He knew, though, that she wasn't seeing him. She was still staring at whatever monster inhabited her dream.

"Lyndon, help me!" she cried.

That was his guess anyway. It was as close as Dixon could get to interpreting the four mumbled syllables. A place deep inside him hitched to hear her call her fiancé's name. His fists clenched at his sides. At least he knew what she was dreaming.

Instinctively, he knew this wasn't the first time she'd had this dream. Obviously she didn't remember the dream—or at least not all of it—when she woke.

She was still staring at him with those glassy, unseeing eyes. Her face was ghostly white in the dimness and her chest rose and fell rapidly with her uneven, gasping breaths.

"Rose?" he said softly. "Rose, wake up, hon. You're dreaming." He touched her shoulder lightly. "Come on, Rose. It's okay. You're safe."

As he watched, her gaze cleared and focused. Then, in the next fraction of a second she sat up and scrambled backward until her back hit the thick, tall headboard of the bed. "No!" she cried, her voice clear and laced with panic. "No! Get away from me. Help!" She held up her hands—those beautiful scarred hands—to protect herself.

He straightened and held out his hands in a palms-up, unthreatening gesture. "Rose, it's me. Dixon," he said. "You were having a bad dream."

She cowered against the headboard and her eyes cast about, as if she were searching for the best route of escape. "Get away from me!" she cried again. "Get away!"

"Okay," he said, backing away from the bed.

"Talk to me, Rose. Are you awake? Do you know who I am?"

Her chin lifted and she frowned at him.

"Remember? I was sleeping down the hall, in your old room. Do you remember who I am?"

"D-Dixon?" she whispered.

"That's right. It's me. You were having a bad dream."

"Bad…" She shook her head, looked at the rain-streaked window, then at the bedroom door.

"Rose," he said softly and held out his arms. "You're safe."

In one smooth, swift motion, she bounded up and off the bed and into his arms.

He embraced her trembling body as she snaked her arms around his bare waist. He held her close, gently caressing her back, whispering into her sweet-smelling hair.

"Sh-shh," he whispered. "It's okay. You're safe." He gently rocked her from side to side, soothing, calming.

Despite the quivering that rocked her, her cotton-covered breasts were soft and firm against his bare chest. Her back under his fingers curved enticingly, a mixture of delicate muscle and soft roundness. He fought to curb the erotic pulses shooting from the skin of his chest, from his fingertips, from his lips that brushed her hair straight to his groin.

He'd never felt anything like the sensation of holding her. He'd had his share of women, but somewhere deep inside, he knew that Rose was different. And knowing that, he realized that he loved her, that he'd loved her from the first moment he'd seen her picture.

Whether she could ever feel the same was irrelevant. He loved her, and he would die to protect her if that was what it took to keep her safe.

She shifted in his arms and he felt the trembling stop. Finally, she was beginning to calm down. But then, her soft, firm flesh began to shimmer beneath his touch. In relaxing, she'd unconsciously molded her body against his. Suddenly, the soft pressure of her belly and thighs against him turned into exquisite torture as his erection stirred and grew.

He shifted, adjusting his stance so her body didn't press quite so uncomfortably against him.

"Dixon?" she whispered.

"Yeah, Rose," he responded. "I'm right here. Are you feeling better?" He slid his hand up and down her back, comforting her, torturing himself.

"I…" She made a little noise that sounded like a muffled giggle. "I forgot you were here. I was…" She paused and looked up at him. "Was I having a nightmare?"

He nodded. "I think so. Do you remember any of it?"

The furrow between her brows deepened for an instant. "I don't think so," she said. "Although—"

Dixon caught her hand and led her back to the bed. He sat and tugged on her hand until she sat, too. "Will you tell me about it? Your dream?"

She shrugged her bare shoulders and he watched the lamplight dance across the delicate bones and muscles of her shoulders and neck. He wanted to taste all the places the light touched. He wanted to taste all the places the light didn't touch—had never touched.

Stop it. He swallowed hard and forced himself to ignore his still-pulsing erection. He hoped to hell Rose hadn't noticed it. He didn't want her to think that he was being guided by base desires. He needed her to trust him and he was pretty damn sure she wouldn't if she knew how much she turned him on.

"I'm not sure I can," she was saying. Dixon had to think back a couple of seconds. She was responding to his request that she tell him about her dream.

"Just talk. Try to verbalize what you do remember, before it gets too far away and you can't."

"Maman would come in and lie down with me when I had the nightmares," she said. "She'd tell me to forget them and go back to sleep."

Dixon ran his thumb across her knuckles, feeling the almost undetectable ridge of a scar. "Is that what you want to do?" he asked softly.

She shook her head, then bent it. Her soft dark hair fell, shadowing her face. "No. Maman was like a sentry, guarding me, keeping the memories at bay. But you…" She lifted her head and met his gaze, her eyes glowing like amber in the pale light. "I somehow feel safer with you."

He felt a slight sting at the back of his eyes. "I swear to you, Rose, you can trust me with your life. I won't let anything or anyone hurt you."

"I believe you," she said as her gaze drifted down from his eyes to his mouth. For an instant, he thought she might kiss him, and for the life of him he didn't know what would happen if she did.

He'd just promised her that she could trust him, but he was sitting next to her on her still-warm bed, clad only in khaki slacks. She wore even less—a thin, gauzy nightgown which might as well not have been there.

Her tongue slipped out to moisten her lips and he nearly lost it. His erection, which he'd thought he had under control, surged to full engorgement.

He stood quickly and stepped over to the window, biting his tongue, hoping the pain would deflate his erection. *Get a grip. You're thirty-six, not seventeen. Exercise your strength. Mind over muscle.*

Staring out the window, he saw that it had

stopped raining, and the moon was peeking out from behind the clouds.

He heard the old bedsprings creak, but before he could turn and head for the door, he felt Rose behind him. She laid a hand on his back between his shoulder blades. Her touch burned him like a brand.

"Dixon, what's wrong?"

Without turning around, he spoke. "This is a really bad idea. You need to go back to sleep and I…" He took a long, shuddering breath. "I need to get out of here."

When he turned toward the door, she caught his arm. "I don't want you to go. I need you."

He closed his eyes and clenched his jaw. "Rose, don't. You don't know what you're doing."

Rose laughed quietly and ran her hand up Dixon's arm to his bicep. His skin was warm and supple, so vibrant, so alive. His was the first, the only bare male skin she remembered ever touching. It was smooth and golden in the pale moonlight, yet so different from hers. Stronger, thicker. And irresistibly sexy.

"I've lost my memory, not my mind," she said. "I know what I'm asking."

Dixon turned and gazed into her eyes. "Do you?" he muttered, his jaw working. "I don't think so." He covered her hand with his and removed it from his arm, then placed it on his belly, above the button on his pants. "Is this what you're asking for?"

Rose was shocked, just like she knew he'd intended. She'd watched movies, read books. She'd discovered—or rediscovered—the feelings coaxed from her body by sexual imagery and description. But she'd never felt a man's belly—softer than his arm or his back, but still rock-hard. She'd never seen an erection—not even covered by fabric.

But she wasn't going to let him frighten her into running away—not without fighting. So she splayed her fingers over his warm satiny skin. The muscles under her hand quivered and contracted. He drew in a sharp breath, and she knew she was going to win.

A frisson of anxiety slid down her spine. She really didn't know what she was doing, just like Dixon had said. All she knew was that something about him drew her, unlike anyone else she had ever known—or at least anyone that she remembered.

"Yes," she murmured, lifting her head so that her mouth was less than an inch from his. "That's exactly what I'm asking for."

His eyes looked black in the dim light, and they stared into hers like dark lasers, burning through to the very core of her. "I don't think so," he said, his warm breath drifting across her lips. "But we'll see."

Then he kissed her. He didn't touch her at all, only held her there with the strength of his kiss. Her hand still rested on his belly and she felt the muscles contract even more as she slid her hand downward, past the button on his pants. Her fingertips encountered crisp hair and even softer flesh. Then the back of her hand brushed the silky, rigid length of him.

She gasped, and so did he. His head jerked back and he searched her face. Looking for fear? For surprise? For triumph?

She closed her eyes and reached for his mouth with hers. She parted her lips slightly and tasted his. With a rush of breath, he opened his mouth and met her exploring tongue with his own.

A moan escaped from her throat as a fierce desire speared her down deep in her core, then spread like fire out her limbs, all the way to her fingertips and toes. Her knees quivered.

Instinctively knowing she was about to collapse, he wrapped his arms around her and molded her body to his. His erection pulsed against her belly and stoked the fire his tongue had sparked.

"Rose—" he breathed "—if you're going to stop me, do it now."

She shook her head. "No," she whispered. "Never."

Then she reached for his mouth again, pressing herself against him, rocking against his hardness.

Something was driving her, something beyond physical desire. She needed this. It terrified her how desperate she was to experience this thing she didn't remember ever doing before. She'd existed in a netherworld draped with mysterious whisperings, lies and impenetrable fog.

Dixon had exposed her to her blank past. She needed him to take her further, to help her prove she was alive. That she was capable of facing the world that Maman had hidden from her.

She took refuge in the delicious recesses of his mouth, immersing herself in the taste of him. He wrapped her in his arms and laid her down on the bed. As he shed his slacks and stretched out beside her, the relief she felt was so sharp it startled her.

She moaned.

"Rose?" he murmured. "Do you want me to stop? I can stop—" He drew a quick breath. "I *can*."

She took his face in her hands and kissed him again and again. "Don't you dare stop," she warned him.

He buried his head in the curve of her neck. She nuzzled his hair.

"I was afraid I'd never find you," he whispered, his voice hoarse.

And she understood. No matter how lost she'd been, he had been there, searching for her. Even though she hadn't remembered herself, he had.

Her heart felt shattered. For the first time, she realized how much she needed to believe him. She knew he meant the words, but was he afraid he'd never close his case? Or was he afraid that he was doomed to live the rest of his life without her?

At that instant he lifted himself on his elbows and gazed down at her. He pushed a strand of hair off her forehead and his fingers got tangled in it. He opened his mouth to say something, then frowned and shook his head.

As apprehension curled through her belly, she started to ask him what was wrong, but he pushed his fingers through her hair and bent his head. But he didn't kiss her—not on the mouth. Instead, he pressed his lips to the scar at her hairline. He kissed every millimeter of the knife wound, from her temple, down her cheek to the curve of her jaw.

Then, with his lips still against it, he whispered to her. "I swear to God I'll find him, Rose. I swear. And when I do, I'll do my best not to kill him on the spot. But I'd like to."

"No, Dixon. Don't even say that." She cupped his cheek in her hand and forced him to look at her. "Stay here with me. Don't think about anything but here and now."

His mouth quirked upward. "I can do that," he said, then lowered his mouth to hers in another breath-stealing kiss.

"I love kissing you," she whispered, pushing her fingers between their mouths and touching his lips with her fingertips. "Your mouth looks so straight and harsh. It's hard to believe your lips feel so gentle and sexy." Her fingers trailed across his cheek. "Not so fond of the stubble, though," she teased.

"No?" He rubbed his cheek against hers.

"Ow," she muttered, and he laughed. She smiled at him. "That's the first time I've seen you laugh," she said.

"No, it's not."

She touched his lips again. "Yes, it is."

"Hmm." He nibbled at the underside of her chin, then ran his tongue down her breastbone.

"Oh," she breathed as he touched her breast, cupping it, his thumb caressing the sensitive tip. Her core throbbed—another new sensation. "Oh, Dixon…"

He pushed the soft, loose nightgown away from the tip of her breast and took it into his mouth. She bit her lip, trying to swallow the cry that pushed at her throat. It escaped as a long, pleasured moan. She hadn't dreamed that such ecstasy could exist.

Dixon spread his legs on either side of Rose's flanks. He sat up and slid the delicate gown off her shoulders and down to her waist. He sucked in a sharp breath through his teeth and felt his jaw tighten.

Crisscrossing her chest and the soft skin of the tops of her breasts were more scars. "No," he hissed, more breath than voice. "Rose, how did you bear it?"

"Don't—" she started.

He shook his head and spread his palms over the ugly, pencil-thin ridges that marred her beautiful skin. "I am so sorry, Rose. I'm so…" He couldn't talk anymore past the lump that was blocking his throat.

Bending over her, he touched his tongue to every single scar. Rose gasped "don't" again, but he ignored her, turning his attention from the scarred skin to the dark areolas of her nipples. He sucked in the entire areola, then slowly let it go. Then he did it again, licking it, then nipping the distended tip with his teeth.

Rose uttered a quiet scream as he turned his attention to her other breast and gave it the same erotic attention. Her back arched, pushing her nipples with their dark areolas upward.

She reached for his shoulders, running her hands over his skin, then up to caress the nape of his neck. She tried to pull him toward her, to kiss him, but he wouldn't cooperate. Instead, he moved down her belly, discovering only one long, jagged scar there. He caressed and soothed it with his tongue as well.

He followed his tongue with his fingers, sliding

them down over her abdomen and farther, until he cupped his palm between her thighs and slowly stroked her.

His touch sang through Rose with the bright hot fury of lightning across a dark summer sky. When he dipped into her with one long finger, pushing in, then withdrawing, pushing and withdrawing, in an erotic parody of lovemaking. He rested his head on her belly, feeling the small rhythmic contractions of her muscles.

She tried to grasp his wrist, tried to stop the sensual assault. "Dixon—" she gasped. "What—"

He stopped.

"No! Don't stop, please," she begged. Opening her eyes, she realized that the moon was shining in the window, turning their flesh an odd silvery gold color.

She'd felt the strength of his body, seen a hint of his smooth golden flesh in the pale rain-soaked streetlamp's light, but now she devoured the planes and bulges, all the places, both smooth and hairy.

He looked leaner without his clothes, but still muscled and hard. His broad chest heaved with his harsh breaths, his abdomen rippled and his thighs flexed powerfully.

He wasn't looking at her face, his attention was on his finger, hidden in the thatch of red-gold hair at the apex of her thighs. He dipped into her again, deeper, and she forgot what she'd been doing— what she'd been thinking.

Nothing mattered, nothing existed but his intimate probing caress. She arched against him, more than ready. He turned to her then, bringing himself back up to kiss her.

Some instinct compelled her to wrap her fingers around his hardness. He threw his head back and a shuddering breath hissed out between his teeth.

Then his gaze met hers as he sank into her slowly, so slowly. His jaw was tense, his mouth slightly open, his breath coming fast and hard.

She gasped as he filled her, afraid and yet hungry for him. This—*this* was what she'd needed. She hadn't known it until this very moment, hadn't been able to imagine anything as exquisitely pleasurable.

He grimaced and for a second she thought he was going to stop. She arched against him, begging for more.

"Dixon," she murmured as her hands reached to press him closer, closer. Then as he finally sank to the hilt, she cried out and lost herself in the bliss of orgasm.

Dixon buried his face in the sweet space between her shoulder and neck, panting as he slowly recovered from the most shattering climax he'd ever experienced.

A whisper of guilt tried to edge its way into his brain, but he pushed it away. There was plenty of time later to regret what he was doing. Right now he just wanted to bask in Rose's warm embrace. He sighed and raised his head to look at her.

Her eyes were closed and her lips were parted. As he watched, she pursed them and blew out what could only be described as a satiated breath.

He smiled and bussed the corner of her mouth. Her lips turned up and she opened her eyes to a slit. She looked at him sidelong for a moment, then her eyes drifted shut again.

"Sleepy," she whispered.

"I know," he responded softly, then lay alongside her and pulled her close, so her head rested on his shoulder. It wasn't long before she was breathing evenly, sound asleep. He closed his eyes and didn't stir until daylight peeked in through the open curtains.

He looked down at the top of her head, where red-gold roots peeked out from her scalp in sharp contrast to the rest of her hair, which was dyed black. He pressed a kiss to her forehead and she murmured something and curled her fingers into the hairs on his chest.

And the guilt hit him—like an uppercut to his chin.

What the hell was he doing? He was supposed

to be protecting her, and what had he done? He'd ended up screwing her.

Even as the word flitted through his brain, he knew it was unfair—to her and to himself. What they'd done deserved so much more than the derogatory word. They'd made love.

That didn't make it right. He should have known better. He did know better, but he couldn't regret it. He'd never experienced anything like it in his life. Making love with her was everything he'd never allowed himself to think about in the twelve years since he'd worked that horrific crime scene.

Abruptly, he was reminded of the awful scars he'd uncovered when he'd lowered her nightgown. Crisscrossed and jagged, their ugliness was made more prominent by the creamy pale beauty of her skin and the perfect round firmness of her breasts.

What kind of monster could cut and scar such lovely, precious skin?

Faintly, from the next room, Dixon heard the muted ring of his cell phone. Grimacing, he slid carefully and quietly out of Rose's bed. She stirred and turned over but didn't wake up.

Tiptoeing out, he pulled her door closed and hurried into the second bedroom. He snatched his phone from the bedside table.

It was Delancey. *Damn it.* Guilt stabbed him again. If—when—his partner found out what he was hiding from him, he'd probably shoot him. If he ever found out that he'd slept with his cousin Rosemary, Dixon knew he'd wish for the swift death promised by a bullet.

Chapter Eleven

"What do you remember about your cousin Rosemary from back then?" Dixon asked his partner as they were driving to the scene of a shooting at the old St. Louis Cemetery, on the corner of St. Louis and Basin Streets. If asked, he couldn't have said why he kept digging at Ethan's memories of his cousin.

Was it hunger to know more about her, or a back-handed attempt to nudge Ethan toward the realization that Rosemary was still alive, without actually having to tell him?

Ethan yawned and took a drink from his paper cup of coffee. "Come on, Dix. Obsessed much? Why are you still on that? Didn't you tell me that T-Bo didn't tell you anything except for Junior Fulbright's name?"

Dixon had been steeped in thoughts of Rose. He forced his attention back to the subject of T-Bo. "Yeah, but now he's been murdered."

"You don't know that it has anything to do with his talking to you."

"It was the same day," Dixon reminded Ethan.

"Exactly," Ethan responded. "Isn't that mighty fast to order and carry out a hit?"

"Maybe, but he had a bar of soap stuffed down his throat. You know what that means."

"Sure. Somebody didn't like something he said—or did—with his mouth. Maybe it was a lover's quarrel."

"I got a list of everyone who visited inmates that day. There were over forty. That plus three hundred phone calls equals a long list of possibles for who might have ordered the hit on T-Bo." He sighed. "And that doesn't count the guards or trustees who might have been involved in getting a message to an inmate."

"You're going to go through all of them? On a hunch?"

Dixon shook his head. "I've asked the warden to take a look and tell me if he's ever had even a whisper of trouble out of any of the names on the lists."

Ethan huffed and drank his coffee.

"I'm serious, Delancey. I want to know about Rosemary. What do you remember about her?"

"And *I'm* serious, Dix. I'm about to get really tired of this. Why in hell can't you stop obsessing over her? She's dead."

"The answer's the same as the last dozen times. In the twelve years I've been a homicide detective, hers is the only case I've never closed."

"Well, get over it, because you're never going to close that one. Hell, Shively was the lead detective and he managed to retire happy without closing it."

Dixon turned onto St. Louis Street and parked at the curb behind one of two patrol cars whose blue lights were flashing. On the other side of the street, an ambulance idled. He killed the engine and then turned to look at Ethan.

"Think about it for a minute. What if T-Bo was telling the truth? What if she's out there—maybe with amnesia or something. What if your cousin was still alive and you did nothing to help her?"

Ethan sent him an *are-you-completely-nuts?* look, then shook his head in exasperation. "I was sixteen when it happened," he said grudgingly. "Rosemary was twenty-two. She was a lifetime older than me—or that's what I thought at the time. I was interested in girls, not cousins."

Dixon waited.

"Rosemary had moved out when she started college, gotten her own apartment. She was majoring in Music, I think, but she did modeling jobs—runway jobs—too."

"Did she have a lot of money? A trust fund? Money from her folks?"

Ethan shook his head. "Our trust funds don't kick in until our twenty-fifth birthday. I'm pretty sure Grandmother paid for her apartment and car. Or maybe Uncle Robert. Why?"

"I'm just trying to figure out why she was targeted. So you're saying she probably couldn't get her hands on a large amount of cash."

"All I can do is tell you what I think now, looking back. I have no idea. Why the question about money anyhow?"

Dixon shrugged. "She was a Delancey. Maybe the murder was about money."

"Her fiancé's money maybe. He was Eldridge Banker's son. Wasn't he killed that night, too?"

Dixon nodded. "Two buildings away from her apartment. We figured he came in, surprised the killer and ran."

"Ran? I don't think I ever knew that. What a guy!"

"Yeah. The killer chased him and shot him in an alley, then dragged his body behind a trash bin. And that's where things get weird."

Ethan eyed him. "You think the killer went back to her apartment and she was gone."

"That's the best guess. Or at least it's my guess. The M.E. never made a ruling because the body was missing. The case is officially still open."

"And there was nothing at the scene that could identify the killer."

"Right."

"No DNA? No trace of any kind? No finger-print?"

Dixon shook his head.

"The killer was that good?"

"I'm just telling you what the M.E. and the crime scene investigators put in their official reports."

"So what happened? You think Rosemary just got up and walked out—totally naked and covered with blood?"

"I don't know. There was a sash for a terry cloth robe…" Dixon stopped. How much could he—should he—tell Ethan? He gave a mental shrug. "The sash appeared to have been used to tie her hands to the bedposts. It was soaked in blood, but CSU never turned up a robe."

Ethan winced at Dixon's words. "Why didn't y'all follow her footprints? She couldn't have gotten very far."

"There was a thunderstorm that night. There weren't any footprints to follow."

Ethan put his coffee in the cup holder and opened the passenger door. Dixon caught up with him. They strode over to join a small crowd.

"All right, folks," Ethan said, holding up his badge. "The show's over. Get out of here or I'll pull you in for loitering."

By the time the crowd had thinned out, the

EMTs had draped a sheet over a body on the ground and loaded a large, unconscious man onto a gurney, rolling it toward the ambulance.

"Hey," Ethan called to the EMTs. "Who you got there?"

The EMT shrugged. "The officers have his wallet. They said we could take him on to the hospital. He's going to need surgery."

Ethan stepped over to the gurney. Dixon followed.

"I know this guy," Ethan said. "He's a bouncer at the Top Hat."

"The topless place on Bourbon?" the younger EMT asked, staring down at the unconscious man with renewed interest. "Wow. Well, he's big enough for sure. Wonder if he did any bouncing with the girls?"

Dixon shot him a disgusted look. "Weren't you on your way to the hospital?" he snapped, then turned to his partner. "You have a history with this guy?"

"I've talked to him a few times, mostly back when I was a patrolman. His name's Gordon Blunt. People call him BFT."

"BFT?" Dixon repeated.

Ethan smirked. "Blunt force trauma. He moonlighted as protection for some of the ladies. I was called to a domestic dispute one night. Girl and her pimp had gotten into it. I couldn't find the pimp, but I took her in to a clinic to get her stitched up. A few days later, I get word the pimp got his ear bitten off."

"And you think it was…" Dixon gestured toward the ambulance that was pulling away.

"I sure do." Ethan turned as the uniformed officer walked up. "Who's that?" he asked, jerking a thumb toward the body.

"Lavonne Dufour," the officer answered, drawing out the name sarcastically. He held up a card. "I'm pretty sure this driver's license is bogus."

"That's him." Ethan grinned. "That's the pimp that got into it with BFT." He lifted the sheet. "Take a look at that ear."

Dixon dutifully leaned over and checked out the dead man's missing ear. It did look like it had been bitten off.

Just then his phone rang. He grabbed it and looked at the display. It was Bing, the café owner. His blood chilled.

"Got to take this," he said, walking away from them. He didn't miss the curious look Ethan gave him.

"Lloyd," he said into the phone.

"Yeah, Detective. I got something for you."

"What is it?"

"There's a guy been hanging around Rose's. Acts like he's part of the neighborhood, but he ain't. Least I've never seen him before."

"What's he doing exactly?"

"Exactly? Smoking lots of cigarettes, watching her door. Talking on his phone."

"I'll be over there as soon as I can."

"I'm gonna try and get a picture of him with my camera."

"Bing, don't. Don't try anything like that. He could be dangerous."

Bing laughed. "I'll be careful," he said, then the line went dead.

"Bing?" Dixon looked at his display. Plenty of bars. Bing had hung up. "Damn it."

He walked back over to where Ethan was making sure the CSI got pictures of the body and the crime scene from all angles and listening to the kid's account of the first time he'd ever been in a topless club.

"I got to go. Got a situation with a—CI."

"Who?" Ethan asked, pocketing his smartphone.

"You don't know him."

"I'll go with you."

Dixon shook his head. "Nope, not this time. Can you get home?"

"Sure, one of the patrolmen will give me a ride." Ethan gave Dixon an odd look. "What's going on with you?" he asked.

Dixon had already turned to head for his car.

"Nothing," he called back over his shoulder. "I'll tell you about it later—if there's anything to tell."

BING SET A cup of café au lait down in front of a sleepy-eyed man in a rumpled suit and wiped his hands on the towel that was draped across his shoulder. As he turned to head back into the kitchen, his gaze lit on Dixon. His brows went up and he stepped over to the table Dixon had chosen because it was nearest to the voodoo shop.

"Didn't see you sit down," Bing said. "Want a café au lait?"

Dixon shook his head. "I'm not going to be here that long. Tell me about the guy."

"I'll do better than that. I got a picture of him." Bing reached into his pants pocket and pulled out his camera.

"I told you not to take that chance," Dixon snapped. "He could be dangerous."

Bing's broad, florid face wrinkled into a scowl. "You also remarked that you bet I could take care of myself. Remember?" He pointed to the tattoo on his left forearm.

"Sure, but—"

"You don't think I stay prepared in this neck of the woods?" Bing cast a sly glance down toward his ample waist. Dixon followed his gaze and saw the vague outline Bing was referring to. He considered himself to be observant but he hadn't spotted the gun until Bing pointed it out.

"Impressive," he said.

"Yeah? Wait 'til you find out what it is," Bing said, grinning. "Then you really will be impressed. It's a SIG SAUER P226."

Dixon murmured agreement. "You got a carry permit?"

Bing gave a one-shouldered shrug.

Dixon sighed. "Okay, never mind. I don't want to know the answer to that. Let's see the picture you took."

Bing glanced around, checking the tables to be sure nobody needed his attention, then he perched on the edge of one of the chairs, if a two-hundred-and-fifty-pound man could be described as perching. He pulled his phone out of his left front pants pocket and pressed a button.

The photo was a long-shot, but Dixon recognized the subject immediately. "Junior," he said disgustedly.

"You know him?" Bing said.

"Yeah. Two-bit punk. I'd jerk a knot in him and send him dragging his tail back to his daddy, if I thought it would do any good."

"You his babysitter?"

Dixon shook his head. "Nah, but he needs one. He's probably going to end up dead." He stood and tossed a five from his pocket onto the table. If Junior was skulking around here, Reed should have been stuck to him like glue.

"Did you see anybody else who looked out of place?"

When Bing shook his head, Dixon was relieved. If Bing, who'd been on the lookout for anyone or anything unusual, hadn't spotted Reed, then Dixon had confirmation of just how good the private investigator was.

Bing picked up the five-dollar bill and held it out. "That's not necessary," he said. "We watch out for each other in this neighborhood."

"Keep it. You can buy me a café au lait next time."

Bing grinned as a young woman at a nearby table waved a hand in the air. "Deal," he said, pocketing the bill.

"And Bing, get a carry permit."

The Marine nodded as he headed toward the woman's table.

Rose squeezed her eyes shut, but she couldn't block out the sun. Opening one eye to a narrow slit, she looked toward the window. What time was it anyway?

Late. That much she knew. Dixon had left before dawn. She'd woken slightly when his cell phone rang, then had gone back to sleep almost immediately once she heard him lock the front door.

She turned over onto her back and stretched luxuriously, enjoying the feel of the cotton sheets against her bare skin. She felt soft, supple, *satiated*.

She shivered as a memory of Dixon holding her, loving her, filling her, sang through her core. It had been exciting and scary, and better than she'd ever imagined sex could be.

She stretched again, sighing contentedly, then laid her head on the pillow. In the middle of a jaw-stretching yawn, she gulped.

She'd gone to bed with Dixon. And although it hadn't seemed natural—after all it was her first time, or the first time she ever remembered—it *had* seemed right.

Right and comfortable and amazing, there in the dark with the rain drumming against the window panes. Dixon had come to her and chased away her nightmares. He'd banished the susurrus whisperings. He'd doused the brilliant, deadly flashes.

But now that she was awake and bathed in bright rational daylight, it seemed reckless of her to have given herself so completely to him. She'd invited into her bed the one man in the world who could ruin her life. He'd already disrupted her safe, quiet existence in ways her imagination had never conceived.

Because of him, she was afraid in her own home for the first time in her memory. Because of him, she'd lost the innocence in which Maman had cloaked her. She'd moved in here after Maman died because sleeping in her own room just made Maman's bedroom feel more empty.

Reluctantly, she threw back the covers and sat up. Her gaze stopped on the closet door. She shivered. She didn't want to think about the blood-stained bathrobe. Not this morning. Her gaze slid to the old armoire. One door was half-open and a white lace shawl was draped over it.

She smiled, remembering Maman telling her stories of the shawls and gowns and gloves as she'd cleaned and bandaged her wounds. There was a story behind every garment and often, Maman would sometimes model them for Rose as she wove her tale. Many of them involved men—prominent businessmen, politicians, musicians.

Rose had no doubt that many of the tales, if not all, were true. Renée Pettitpas had undoubtedly been a lovely, desirable woman. Even in her late seventies, her face had held an imperial beauty.

What would she say if she knew Rose had slept with the detective who'd investigated her murder? She didn't have to ask that question. She knew what Maman Renée would say.

She'd be furious that Rose had allowed Detective Lloyd into her house—into her bed. *I worked to make you safe within these walls.*

That thought sobered Rose. She fished her nightgown out from the sheets and pulled it over her head, then slipped on a pink kimono that lay across a chair.

She walked over to the armoire and opened the right-hand door where Maman's shawls and scarves hung. She lifted an ivory lace shawl with long fringe from a hanger and wrapped it around herself, breathing in the scent of lavender that clung to it.

"Why did you try so hard to shield me from the truth?" she whispered. "Did you think you could protect me forever?" Her eyes filled with tears. She knew Maman had done what she'd thought was best, but she'd left Rose ill-prepared for the truth.

"Did you know?" she murmured. "Did you know who I was the whole time? Did you keep the truth from me for my sake—or yours?"

DIXON DIALED REED'S number as he walked down the street toward the voodoo shop. It was nearly nine o'clock in the morning, but he didn't see any signs of life from the second-floor windows. Shouldn't Rose be up by now? Maybe teaching a piano lesson?

"Reed," a strong baritone voice said. "Reed, it's Detective Dixon Lloyd."

"Yes?" The voice took on a deliberately neutral tone.

"Can't talk?"

"Right. Thanks," Reed said. "I'll get back to you."

Dixon hung up, frustrated. He wanted to find out from Reed what Junior had been doing in this part of town, but he appreciated Reed's caution.

He pocketed his phone and studied Rose's windows—the big picture window in the living room and to the left of it, the two bedroom windows. Just a few hours ago, he'd made love with her in that middle room. And he'd stood at that window, looking out at the rain.

Had Junior been out here watching him? Dixon hadn't noticed anyone lurking around under the streetlamps, but then his mind hadn't exactly been on surveillance at the time.

He growled under his breath. He'd been distracted—to say the least. Setting his jaw, he renewed his vow to protect Rose.

Protect her. That meant *no* distractions. *None.* For the time being, maybe forever, he had to lock away his desire, his love, and treat her as he would any victim of a heinous crime. His feelings would not—could not—get in the way. Feelings were a distraction and the slightest distraction could get people killed. His parents had been in the middle of an argument when they'd driven off in their car that fateful day. Dixon had been old enough to understand that they'd died because they'd been distracted.

His phone vibrated in his pocket. When he moved to answer it, he realized his fists were clenched and he was still staring up at Rose's window. He shook out his cramped fingers and answered.

"Reed here. Sorry about before."

"Junior was spotted here on Prytania," Dixon said without preamble.

"Right. We were there all night. We got a nice view of you around four or so this morning."

Dixon winced. Just as he'd feared. If Reed had seen him at Rose's window, then so had Junior.

"Bing, the owner of the sidewalk café, got a picture of Junior but he didn't mention seeing you," Dixon commented.

"That's because I'm good."

Dixon acknowledged Reed's statement with a slight pause. "So what have you found out about him?"

"When he left class just before noon yesterday, he headed over to an old office building off Canal," Reed said. "I didn't follow him inside because I didn't know the building, but I've got a list of the businesses that operate from there. Should I send it to you or would you rather meet? I've annotated the list."

"Send it. What's the address?"

Reed gave him an address on Tchoupitoulas Street.

"I know that building. A couple of loan sharks operate out of there. And an escort service we busted for prostitution a couple of years ago."

"Yep. It's a Who's Who of minor crime lords. Even Tito Vega from over on the Mississippi Coast rented office space in there until he went to prison. There's a For Rent sign on his suite now."

"And you don't know which office Junior visited?"

"Nope. I'm sending you the list of names now. So do I stay on Junior?"

"Nope. Thanks. I'll take over for now."

"If you need me again, you know how to reach me," Reed said and disconnected.

Dixon hung up and considered what Reed had told him. Whoever Junior had gone to see yesterday had told him to tail Rose. He'd spent the night watching Rose's house.

A soft chime from his phone indicated that he'd received a message. A second chime sounded as he looked at the display.

Reed had forwarded him two lists. The first was the directory of businesses occupying space in the building on Tchoupitoulas. The second was Junior Fulbright's class schedule.

Dixon knew what he had to do. There was no longer the option of sparing his partner's feelings. He had to find out who Junior answered to.

And to do that, he was going to have to bring him in for questioning.

He turned toward his car, but something made him glance back one more time at the bedroom window. At that instant the sun went behind a cloud.

He squinted. Rose stood there, partially obscured by the glass, her black hair in stark contrast to the pale gown she wore. She wasn't looking down at the street. Her head was lifted toward the sun. He stood mesmerized.

Even distorted by glass and half-hidden in shadow, she was the most beautiful thing he'd ever seen. His throat closed and his eyes stung just looking at her.

The sun came out again and reflected off the window panes. Dixon swallowed hard. He couldn't leave without seeing her.

Checking on her, he corrected himself. He needed to remind her to be careful.

It was his duty, after all, to keep her safe.

He strode up to the house and rang the doorbell. He waited, knowing it would take her a minute or so to come down the stairs. He saw her through the cut glass inset in the door.

When she opened the door, he almost gasped. Her hair was in a long single braid. Her cheeks were pink where his beard had rubbed them. They matched the pink floor-length kimono she wore. She was breathtaking.

He blinked and set his jaw. He had to guard against those kinds of feelings if he was going to have a prayer of keeping her safe. Feelings clouded judgment. Distractions could kill.

"Dixon!" she said, her face lighting up.

He frowned and pushed past her. "Close the door."

"What's the matter?" she asked, worry creeping into her voice.

He turned and scowled at her. "You shouldn't be opening your door to just anybody. Wait before you unlock it. Ask who it is. Ask for proof to be sure they're who they say they are."

She angled her head and laughed. "Dixon, I can tell it's you through the glass."

That made sense, but still. "If you don't know the person, please, don't open the door."

"Okay," she said, the laughter still in her voice but fading. "Has something happened?"

He shook his head. "I just wanted to check on you...."

Her smile grew again. "I'm fine," she said, her

amber eyes twinkling. "How about you?" She stepped closer, obviously expecting a kiss.

He ached to kiss her. He couldn't believe how isolated he felt without her lips on his, without her body pressed against his. But if he started kissing her, he couldn't trust himself to stop. And that was not a good idea. Not now. Not until he was one-hundred percent sure she was safe. He took a step backward.

"There is something the matter. What is it?" she asked. "What's happened?"

"Nothing," he snapped, and regretted it when he saw a twinge of hurt cross her face. "Nothing has happened, and I intend to see that nothing does. My job is to make sure you're safe. There's a time and a place for feelings. Right now, you're in danger."

"A time and a place… I don't understand."

"Last night was a mistake. An error in judgment. As long as you're in danger, I can't afford the distraction—"

He was making things worse. He could tell that she was confused and hurt by what he was saying. As he watched, she straightened and lifted her chin.

"I see," she said. "Well, I can't tell you how much I appreciate your concern."

"Rose—" He lifted his hand to the scar at her

temple, but she recoiled slightly. "My priority is your safety. Surely you can understand that."

"I don't think so," she bit out. "Your priority is closing your case. At least you could be honest about it. But don't worry, I'll be careful."

"Please, Rose, trust me. I swear, when all this is over—"

"Don't," she said, holding up her bare hands. The hands he'd kissed and licked and soothed last night. "Please don't make promises you have no intention of keeping. Trust me, I will definitely think twice before I open my door—to anyone."

She whirled and opened the door, making a sweeping gesture. "Goodbye, Detective."

He started to argue, started to grab her shoulders and force her to understand what he was trying to say. But looking at the determined lift of her chin, he decided that it was probably better this way. She was angry with him, and if being angry with him made her more cautious about her safety, then he'd accomplished his goal.

There would be time later to make up for hurting her.

Chapter Twelve

Rose checked her watch again. Thomas should have been there by now. His piano lesson was at three-thirty. But sometimes his mother, who worked night shift as a nurse in the emergency room of Touro Infirmary, had to work a double shift and stay until after four o'clock. That meant his dad, who was an auto mechanic, would have to take him to work with him. Usually one of them would call her to let her know Thomas couldn't be there.

Rose had offered several times to keep Thomas, but his mother hadn't wanted to impose.

"If you'd let me keep him, he wouldn't have to miss," Rose muttered irritably as she walked into the kitchen. She set a glass of water down in the porcelain sink so hard that it shattered and cut her palm and the pad of her thumb.

"Ow, damn it," she cried, grabbing a paper towel to press against the cut.

This was all Dixon's fault. Him and his self-righteous pompousness. *Can't let feelings enter in,* he'd said.

Well, if he'd been blocking his feelings the night before, then he was a real expert. Had he felt nothing when he'd whispered "I thought I'd never find you"?

Had he been thinking of nothing more than her safety when he'd made love to every inch of her body? When he'd cried over the scars that crisscrossed the skin of her breasts and stomach?

Had he been *doing his job* when he'd held her close and soared with her to a height of ecstasy she wouldn't have believed possible?

She knew he hadn't. Something Maman had once told her came to her. "Men always think they have a duty to protect women. It's a good excuse that lets them avoid admitting that they care." *I hope you're right, Maman. Remember, you also told me my safety would lie in the hands of the Fool.*

Rose held her hand under the cold water tap. The water made the cut sting, but Rose wasn't thinking about the pain. She was staring at the pink-stained water that swirled in the white porcelain sink, spinning like a pink transparent pinwheel as it ran down the drain. As she watched it, mesmerized, a grating voice echoed in her ear.

Rissshhhh, rozzzzzsss. Rissshhhh, rozzzzzsss. Rissshhhh, rozzzzzsss.

The sound of the doorbell startled her. How long had she been staring at the bloody water? She shut the tap off as the bell rang again, insistently.

"I swear, Dixon, if that's you, I'm not opening the door."

As she started down the stairs, she composed her features. It was probably Thomas, and she didn't want to throw the door open with a scowl on her face.

The distorted figure on the other side of the ruby-and-beveled glass was too tall to be Thomas, and it wasn't Dixon's long, lean frame. But it could be Thomas's dad.

By the time all that had sifted through her brain, she'd gotten to the bottom of the stairs and was reaching for the door.

Dixon's words echoed through her brain as she turned the knob. *You shouldn't be opening your door to just anybody. Ask for proof.*

She tossed her head to rid herself of Dixon's imperious voice as she swung the door open. If he was so concerned about her safety, maybe he should have stuck around to screen her visitors.

She refused to be afraid in her own home, in her own neighborhood.

The man standing at the door smiled when Rose's gaze met his. She had two fleeting thoughts. The first was that with his close-set black eyes, flat nose and sallow skin, and those small yellow teeth, he looked like an alligator. The second was that there was something familiar about him.

"Yes?" she said politely yet coolly, frowning slightly as she studied his face.

"Ms. Pettitpas?" he said with a slight bow.

Alarm skittered through her. The low, harsh voice grated like a rusty hinge. Pain jabbed through her temples. Had she heard it before?

"No, I'm sorry," she said, and stepped backward. As she pushed the door into the jamb and felt the resistance of wood against wood, something crashed into her, cracking her head and knocking her backward.

"No!" she shrieked as her hip, her elbow, then the back of her head, slammed into the hardwood floor. Blue-white fireworks exploded before her eyes. Her head ached abominably, and her hip and elbow throbbed.

She fought through the pain, but her temples were still reverberating from the blow as she twisted onto her stomach and started crawling away from the man. She tried to scream for help.

"Come on, Rosemary, don't make this difficult," the man said. "I have a job to do." As he talked, he stepped up to her.

She'd managed to push herself up to her hands and knees, but he planted his feet on either side of her sprawled figure and grabbed her hair in his fist. "Be good, Irish Rose."

Through the pain-filled haze in her brain, she heard the whispers that filled her nightmares.

Rissshhhh, rozzzzzsss. Rissshhhh, rozzzzzsss. Rissshhhh, rozzzzzsss.

"No-o-o!" she wailed. It was him. He was back and he was going to kill her.

She tried to jerk away, but his grip was like iron. "Please, no."

"Well, look at that. The door cut your forehead," the man was saying as he held her by the hair. "I didn't enjoy torturing you before and I certainly don't want to now. Luckily that cut will leave plenty of blood behind for your Detective Lloyd, won't it, Rose?"

Rissshhhh, rozzzzzsss. Rissshhhh, rozzzzzsss.

She jerked her head, trying to dislodge his hand from her hair, but he jerked her head backward, bringing tears of pain to her eyes.

"Let go of me!" she cried.

"Soon, Rosemary. Soon. If you cooperate, things will go much more smoothly. If not, well…" He pulled a taser from his pocket."

Rose went rigid. "What is that?"

"This? It's a taser. Don't you watch TV? It's the latest technology for making people do what you want them to do."

Just as the word *taser* registered in her brain,

she heard a sizzling sound and her whole body felt as if it were on fire.

Her muscles seized in cramping pain, then went limp, all within a fraction of a second. She collapsed to the floor, hitting her forehead again, and blacked out.

Aron Wasabe looked at the woman sprawled on the floor, then at the taser. "Nice," he said. "Exactly as advertised."

He studied Rosemary's sprawled body. His gut reaction when she'd opened the door had been that Junior was wrong. This wasn't Rosemary Delancey.

But it hadn't taken but a millisecond for him to see that of course it was her. Nothing could obscure that haughty, regal beauty.

Yes, her hair was black, but now he saw the pale roots—a kind of reddish gold, the same color as her eyebrows.

He reached down and grabbed a fistful of her hair to turn her face upward. There was the slender ridge of scar that ran from her hairline down to the curve of her jaw.

His work. His fingers twitched. Even after all this time, he remembered the feel of the knife in his hand. He still felt the same mixture of revulsion and raw excitement as he recalled how the ultrasharp blade had split her skin. A faint shudder rocked him and his stomach churned with nausea.

He preferred a knife because it was clean and precise. He'd made a career of dispatching his assignments with one stroke.

The memory of torturing Rosemary Delancey had haunted him for twelve years. Wasabe frowned. He wasn't sure how he would react if The Boss told him to do it again.

While those thoughts swirled in his head, he pushed her legs out of the way and closed the front door. Sure enough, like many people, she'd left the keys in the dead bolt lock for convenience. He locked the door, then pocketed the keys. Digging a roll of elastic bandage out of his pocket, he quickly bound her hands and feet. The Boss's instructions were very specific. No tape burns, no ligature marks. No sign whatsoever that she had been restrained. He had no idea why, but if The Boss wanted it, fine.

From another pocket, he pulled a small roll of paper tape, the type used in hospitals for sensitive skin. He pressed it tightly over her mouth. The tape shouldn't bother her skin, but just to be sure, he'd take it off as soon as he got her to the warehouse.

Just as he finished, her eyes opened. They were glassy and unfocused. It was almost comical to watch her limbs twitch uncontrollably as she struggled against her bindings.

He jolted her again with the taser. With a

strangled moan, she crumpled like a dropped marionette. He nudged her arm with his foot, but it flopped in a way that nobody could fake. She was out.

He quickly walked past her toward the side door at the back of the house. It was locked, but the front door key opened it easily. Outside the door was a narrow concrete stoop with two steps down to the shell-and-gravel alleyway.

Wasabe walked around the house to his car and backed it into the alley. Then he dragged Rosemary through the rooms, out the side door and down the steps. He stopped to catch his breath before hefting her into the car's trunk. It had been years since he'd had to move a deadweight. He wasn't used to the heavy work anymore.

He'd disabled the trunk release as soon as he'd bought the four-door sedan several years ago. It was registered under the name of Aron Accounting, the shell business he'd set up back when he'd had to do his own heavy lifting. Nowadays, part of the exorbitant fee he demanded paid for underlings to handle disposal.

Disposal. Something he hadn't had a chance to do with Rosemary or her fiancé. That first job had been a fiasco from the start. He never should have taken it, but he'd been young and green and willing to take the dirty jobs because that was how a skinny kid from Chicago got noticed in the dank dark underbelly of New Orleans.

Over the years he'd developed a useful set of skills, which had made him one of the most sought-after hit men in the southeastern United States.

He'd become somewhat of a legend for his skill with a balisong, also called a butterfly knife. Its advantage was that it could be opened and ready to use with one hand. He liked it better than a switchblade because few people had ever seen one and were caught completely off guard when he slung it open. But even more than the ease of handling, he liked the symmetry of it. The way the handles swung in opposing arcs from around the blade.

Seeing the amateurish knife work on Rosemary Delancey's face was shocking and repulsive to him. She'd been his first actual hit, and she'd taught him a lot.

First and foremost, only take jobs guaranteed to be quick and clean. He'd vowed that night to never accept a job that required him to torture a subject. The Beauty Queen Murder had made his career, as The Boss routinely reminded him. But while he never fretted over the people he killed, he'd never gotten over what he'd done to Rosemary.

Now, finally, he was delivering the goods to The Boss. Once he fulfilled this obligation and put his guilt to rest, he was hanging up his knife. He'd made enough money so that he didn't have to work ever again. He could retire, and let Wexler take complete control of Aron Accounting.

Wasabe could putter in his yard, go fishing, never miss his little girl's soccer games. Maybe they'd even have another baby.

Wasabe started the car, grabbed a pair of dark glasses from the visor and put them on, then pulled out of the alley. As he did, he saw a child with a manila envelope under his arm, knocking on Rosemary Delancey's front door.

When the boy saw the car, his brows furrowed and his hand raised in an almost-wave.

Wasabe changed his game plan within the blink of an eye. He'd planned to head west on Prytania to get back to St. Charles. He doubted that the kid, who looked no older than nine, would even think about memorizing the license plate, but just in case, he didn't want to give him enough time.

So he turned east instead and took an immediate right. That way, the kid, or anyone else who might be looking, had only a five- or six-second view of the back of the vehicle before it turned.

Wasabe looked in his rearview mirror as he turned. The kid had stepped into the street and was watching his car.

He drove out Gentilly Street to Chef Menteur Highway. Several miles out Chef Menteur were some warehouses that had been damaged in Katrina. Aron Accounting had purchased one a few years ago that from the outside appeared to be destroyed. Inside, however, the steel frame was intact and there were only a couple of places where the roof leaked. He stored things there that he didn't want to keep at home, including the car.

And that's where he'd keep Rosemary until The Boss was ready for her.

Up ahead was the turn for the warehouse. He took a right off Chef Menteur and wound around the freight roads to the front of the building, which faced a small canal. After pulling into the shade of the building, he dialed The Boss on a throwaway cell phone.

"The package is in storage," he said.

He heard The Boss suck in a deep breath. "I can't get away until late. Keep it secure. I'll call you."

"My kid's got a soccer game, so I'll be back here—"

"Your kid will have to play without you."

Wasabe frowned. "Wait a minute. I don't miss my little girl's games. You know that."

"This time you do, if you know what's good for you. You let her slip through your fingers this time, you won't have any left." The Boss hung up.

Wasabe's breath hissed out between his teeth. "I'm not missing the soccer game," he muttered.

"Not even for you." But even while he was furious at The Boss for ordering him around, he breathed a sigh of relief. He'd been afraid The Boss would order him to work on her. He wouldn't have been able to say no.

After all, he'd failed The Boss last time.

THE SECOND LIST Reed had sent Dixon placed Junior in an English Literature class at two o'clock and a Biology lab at four. If Dixon timed it right, he could LoJack Junior's car, go check on Rose and get back before the lab was over.

When Dixon drove by Junior's apartment around three-fifteen, his car wasn't there. So Dixon headed over to Delgado Community College and checked around the English building. Sure enough, he spotted it. He hung around until class let out and followed Junior home. As soon as the punk was inside his apartment, Dixon quickly LoJacked his car.

He checked his watch. He had an hour and a half to drive over to Prytania and check on Rose.

She'd been so angry this morning. He'd known as soon as he'd opened his mouth that she hadn't understood what he was trying to tell her. And the more he'd talked, the worse it had gotten.

He'd decided he had to use her piano students as leverage. He should have yesterday. She wouldn't refuse to go with him if by staying, she thought she was putting her students at risk.

His phone rang. A glance told him it was the crime lab.

"Detective Lloyd? This is Bearden at the crime lab. I've got the results on that robe you brought in on Monday."

Dixon's heart rate tripled. "Yeah?"

"The blood type is a match for Rosemary Delancey. And the fabric is a match for the terry cloth sash that was found at the scene."

Relief washed over him. It was proof—legal proof that Rose was Rosemary Delancey. Now he had more than just his own conviction. She *was* Rosemary Delancey.

Now if he could just catch the man who had tried to kill her.

"Detective?"

The criminalist's voice reminded Dixon that he was still on the phone. "Yeah? Is there something else?"

"Yes, sir. I've got a second blood type on the robe."

"A second— Are you telling me—"

"Can't say for sure, of course," the criminalist continued. "But it could be her attacker's blood. She might have scratched him or he might have cut himself with his own knife. Most people who use a knife to attack someone end up cutting themselves as well."

"Thanks," Dixon said. "Good work." He parked at the curb and stuck his phone back into his jacket pocket as he walked up to Rosemary's door. Suddenly, he had a whole new outlook on the day. He couldn't wait to tell her that the robe had turned up irrefutable proof that she was Rosemary Delancey. He couldn't wait to wipe the doubt and fear from her eyes.

He rang Rose's doorbell and listened to the peals echo through the house as if it were empty. Dread chased away his good mood. Where was she? He rang the bell again and again. Then he knocked loudly. Finally, he used the key Rose had given him.

Slipping inside, he started toward the stairs. "Rose?" he called, just as his foot slipped on something wet. He looked down.

What he saw enveloped his heart in a deep, sick horror, like nothing he'd ever experienced. The hardwood floor was streaked with blood. He swayed and caught himself on the doorjamb. He leaned there for a few seconds, until the nauseating haze finally cleared from his brain and eyes. He wiped a hand down his face, smearing cold sweat across his skin, then finally, after a deep fortifying breath, he forced himself to look at the floor again.

It was definitely blood—and still wet. Dixon immediately drew his weapon. Quickly and carefully, he searched the first floor, then the second. When he was sure the house was empty, he came back downstairs and bent to study the blood-streaked wood more closely.

For an instant, he stared at the sight that mirrored the bloody crime scene from twelve years ago. Blinking and shaking his head, he forced himself to think logically, like a police detective.

The amount of blood was actually minimal. Except for the fact that it was smeared and there were a pair of scrapes running through it, he could have believed that Rose had cut herself on a piece of glass or a splinter of wood.

He fished his high-powered flashlight out of his pocket and studied the scrapes more closely. They were faint, having only scratched the top layer of polish off the wood. He stood and followed their path with his gaze. The two lines were parallel and ran essentially straight back through the house until they disappeared into darkness.

He knew exactly what the scrapes were. The backs of a small pair of boot heels had scratched the glossy surface as someone had dragged the wearer.

Fear wrapped icy fingers around his heart as his brain replayed what must have happened. Someone, Junior's boss probably, had rung the doorbell.

When Rose opened the door, he'd incapacitated her, maybe with a taser or ether or some other fast-acting, inhaled anesthetic. He swallowed against nausea.

Or a knife.

Whatever the means, the attacker had made sure she couldn't fight him, then he'd dragged her to the back door. But what had happened to cause the blood? There was so little of it. Barely enough to see. Had Rose scratched her attacker?

His hand automatically went to the pocket of his jacket where he always carried a pair of gloves. Then it hit him.

The blood was a message, to him. He'd been there in that bloody apartment. The monster who had taken Rose was the same person who'd cut her before. He'd spilled Rose's blood as a message to Dixon.

"I'll get you, bastard. You'll pay for hurting her," he muttered as he walked through the long, narrow first floor of the house, following the parallel marks all the way to the back door. It was standing open. He stepped outside onto the concrete stoop. Sure enough there were two scrapes marring the concrete, identical to the ones in the house.

Stepping down onto the shell-and-gravel driveway, he spotted tire tracks. Fresh ones. He hugged the side of the house as he studied them. He'd dragged her back here and out the door, stuffed her into his car, probably his trunk, and taken off.

Pulling out his phone, he called Dispatch.

"This is Detective Dixon Lloyd," he told the dispatcher and recited his badge number. "I've got a home invasion and possible abduction." He quickly recited the address and named Rose Bohème as the victim.

As he hung up, a voice called to him.

"Hey, mister!"

When he turned, he saw a boy around nine years old rounding the corner of the house, followed by a tired-looking woman with a dish towel in her hand.

"Thomas, come back here," the woman called, but the boy didn't listen to her. "Thomas!" she called again.

"Whoa," Dixon said, holding up a hand as he walked toward the boy. "Hold it. Don't mess up those tire tracks."

"No, sir," the boy said, hugging the wall. "I mean yes, sir. Are you the detective?"

Dixon's brows rose. "Thomas, is it? I'm Detective Dixon Lloyd. How'd you know?"

Thomas stopped in front of Dixon and glanced around. "Everybody knows you've been bothering Miss Rose."

Dixon didn't know what to say to that.

"So, Mr. Detective, I need to tell you what happened. I was s'posed to have a piano lesson, but Miss Rose didn't come to the door." Thomas took a deep breath. "Then I seen somebody had backed a car into the alley there. About the time I was banging on the door, in case Miss Rose's doorbell was broke, that car—it burned rubber pulling out of there." He gestured behind him toward the road.

"Did you see Miss Rose?"

"Nope."

"Thomas—" his mother admonished. "I'm sorry, Detective. Thomas, come with me right now. We need to leave the detective alone so he can work."

"Mom, wait. He asked me to help. I didn't see Miss Rose, but I think she was in the car."

Thomas looked Dixon in the eye, really getting into his theory. "In the trunk. I think the man dragged her out the back door. He probably drugged her to keep her quiet."

"Thomas!" his mother cried, but Dixon held up a hand.

"What makes you think that?"

"Because she's always here. Always, plus nobody ever parks their car in the alley. Not ever."

It was nine-year-old reasoning. Simple but sound. Dixon couldn't argue with Thomas's logic. "I see. Can you tell me anything about the car?"

Thomas shrugged. "I don't know much about

cars. It was black and big. It wasn't an SUV. It had a trunk."

Dixon caught Thomas's mother's eye over his head. "Thanks, Thomas. That helps a lot. Now go on back to your house with your mom. I'll call you if I need any more information."

"Come on, Thomas," his mother said, and held out her hand.

"Mom, wait! I've got to tell him—"

"Thomas!"

Dixon regarded the boy. He seemed desperate to tell Dixon his last bit of information. So he sent the boy's mother a nod. "Okay, Thomas, what else?"

"I got the car tag, or at least most of it," Thomas said, lifting his chin and puffing out his chest.

Dixon's breath caught and his pulse hammered. "You did?" he said, hardly daring to believe that the boy had actually memorized the license plate. He sent up a quick prayer. "What was the number?"

Thomas rattled off the number. "I'm good with numbers. Mom, tell him."

Dixon's pulse thudded in his ears. The sequence was right for a Louisiana tag. "Way to go, Thomas! I'm going to have to see that you get a commendation for bravery."

"Really? A condation? Mom, I'm going to get a condation!"

"I know, sweetheart. I heard," she said, her eyes on Dixon's, questioning.

He knew what she wanted to ask him. "I think Miss Rose is going to be all right," he said. "But until we're sure, everybody needs to stay safe. Lock your doors. Let the police know of any suspicious people you see hanging around. And Thomas," he put his hands on Thomas's shoulders, "you need to protect your mom. So don't go running around without her. Okay? Stay near your mom and keep her safe."

Thomas straightened. "Yes, sir." He sent Dixon a sly look. "I probably shouldn't go to school, should I? I need to stay home and protect my mom."

Dixon smiled. "I'm pretty sure your mom will be okay while you're in school. Right now, I need you to take her back home and make sure you keep the doors locked. Okay?" He sent a brief nod to the boy's mom.

"Thank you, Detective," she said. "Come on, Thomas. Let's go."

As they walked up the sidewalk toward their house, Dixon heard sirens. He glanced at his watch. It was after four. As much as he wanted to stay there and work the scene, he knew he needed to get back to the school so he could pick up Junior when he got out of class. He was more convinced than ever that Junior knew who had taken Rose.

As two police cruisers roared up, sirens blasting, a vintage black Camaro pulled up behind them and his partner jumped out.

"Dix, what the hell? You called this in? What are you doing down here?"

"I could ask you the same thing."

"Somebody told me you called in a home invasion over here on Prytania. I figured I'd better come see what you'd got yourself into."

"I don't have time to talk. I've got to be somewhere."

"I'll go with you."

Dixon actually considered that for about half a second. But he wasn't ready to explain everything to Ethan. It would take too long, and he couldn't let Junior slip out of his hands.

He shook his head. "Sorry. I'll fill you in when I get back to the station."

"Dix!"

Dixon opened his car door, then glanced back at Ethan. "Write this down." He recited the license plate number.

Ethan scowled, but grabbed a pen from his pocket and wrote on his palm.

"Kid named Thomas—he lives two doors that way—" Dixon jerked his head. "He can verify the tag. He saw the vehicle. May be able to give you a description of the driver."

"What vehicle? Dix, get back here!"

But Dixon had jumped into his car and cranked it. In his rearview mirror, he saw Ethan standing with his fists on his hips, glaring at him as he pulled away from the curb and took off toward Delgado Community College.

Chapter Thirteen

Dixon double-parked in front of the science building just about the time the double doors crashed open and kids poured out. He spotted Junior, shuffling along in skinny, ground-dragging jeans and talking to a girl in full Goth garb.

He was already frantic with worry about Rose, so waiting while the two of them ambled in the general direction of his car was torture. His hands clenched into fists around the steering wheel so tightly that he had to consciously work at relaxing them.

He waited until they were about to pass the car he was parked alongside, then he climbed out, his badge in his hand.

"Hey, Junior," he said, exercising admirable restraint, because what he wanted to do was throw the punk down on the sidewalk and cuff him. "Got a minute?"

Junior balked and the Goth girl, who was fishing a cigarette out of her purse, almost ran into him. "Hey…" she started, then looked up. Her gaze snapped to Dixon's badge. She froze.

He could tell by the look in Junior's eyes that he was considering making a run for it. "Don't do it, Junior. Remember last time?"

"I got away," Junior mumbled.

"Hah. Barely. And you won't this time."

Junior met Dixon's gaze and his eyes grew wide and round. His skinny neck moved as he swallowed.

"Hey, man," the Goth girl said. "You got business with Junior, that's fine. But I gotta get out of here." She made a show of looking at her large, black, steel-banded watch. "I'm late for—"

Dixon glared at her. "Go on, sugar," he said, and she went—fast. He turned to Junior.

"Where's Rose and who's got her?"

The punk still had that fight-or-flight look in his eyes, but his Birkenstocks were rooted to the sidewalk.

"Huh? I mean—who?" Junior mumbled.

Dixon grabbed a fistful of Junior's T-shirt and lifted him to his tiptoes. "You know who," he growled, his face no more than two inches from the kid's. "The woman you were watching all night."

"What? I didn't do nothing," he whined. "You're hurting me."

"You're going to be hurt if you don't start answering questions." Dixon tightened his fist and lifted the skinny punk completely off the ground.

"Hey, man!" Junior pushed at Dixon's fist with his hands. "Lemme go!"

A man in a suit started toward them, his face filled with concern. Dixon held up his badge. The man nodded, looking relieved, and turned in the other direction.

Dixon dragged Junior over to the passenger door of his car, opened it and thrust him inside. He slammed the door.

Junior eyed the door handle, then looked up at Dixon, but Dixon shook his head and slid his jacket back enough so that the edge of his holster was visible. That got the punk's attention. He folded his arms and settled back against the seat.

Dixon walked around the front of the car, still showing his weapon, and got in on the driver's side.

"Come on, man, don't take me in. My dad's gonna kill me," Junior whined.

"*I'm* going to kill you if you don't give me some answers," Dixon tossed back at him as he pressed the child-safety locks on the doors. Then he cranked the car and headed toward the station. "Now shut up and put your seat belt on."

"You don't understand, man," Junior said brokenly. "He'll let me rot in jail this time."

Dixon glanced in the rearview mirror. The kid

was genuinely terrified. As he drove to the station house, he kept an eye on him. When Junior dug a cell phone out of his pants, Dixon said, "Give me that."

"No, man, I gotta—"

"Give it to me or I'll pull the car over and take it."

"It's my phone—"

"It's not your phone. It's your daddy's because he pays the bills." He met Junior's gaze in the mirror. "And he gave me permission to confiscate it. He's worried about who you've been talking to."

It was a lie, but a calculated one. He doubted Junior would challenge him on it. Junior didn't say anything else; he just pitched the phone over the seat. Dixon pocketed it.

At the station house, Dixon hauled Junior up the stairs and into the squad room. Ethan was back and sitting at his desk.

He stuck Junior in Interrogation Room One and told him to sit tight. Ethan stopped him outside the door and got in his face.

"All right, Dix, what's going on?" Ethan asked, nodding toward the door. "Who's that?"

Dixon had known, ever since he'd first laid eyes on Rose, that this moment would come. But explaining to Ethan wasn't his top priority. Finding Rose was.

"Give me a minute," he said, walking past him

and heading to the computer tech's desk. He handed the tech Junior's phone. "I need to know who these numbers belong to," he told him.

"Sure," the tech responded and set the phone down on the edge of his desk.

"Now!"

The tech looked up. His bored expression turned to apprehension when he met Dixon's gaze. "Okay," he mumbled, picking up the phone.

Dixon returned to where Ethan was standing. "What did they find at the scene?" he asked.

"Damn it, Dix." Ethan scowled. "You can't just go running off from a crime scene. And please don't tell me you think the woman's supposed disappearance has anything to do with my cousin."

Dixon didn't meet Ethan's gaze. "What did the crime scene techs say?"

Ethan's breath whooshed out in a frustrated sigh. "The door wasn't forced—"

"I know that," Dixon interrupted.

"Do you want to know what they said or not?" Ethan snapped back at him.

Dixon clamped his jaw and inclined his head.

"There were no signs of a struggle, but CSI figured the woman was dragged to the back door and put into a vehicle, which left the scene—"

"Did you talk to Thomas? Get the license plate?"

Ethan was so angry that Dixon wouldn't have

been surprised if smoke had come out of his ears, but his police training kept him from blowing up at Dixon—so far.

"He's *nine*," Ethan spat.

"But he got the number, right?" Dixon responded.

Ethan's lips flattened. "It belongs to an Aron Accounting Firm. Company car."

"Aron Accounting? That was one of the names on the building directory. Did they send someone to talk to them? Who's handling the questioning?"

"Dix. Slow down! What build—" Ethan bit off the word. "What the hell is going on?"

Dread and relief mingled inside Dixon. "Let's go in there." He gestured toward Interrogation Room Two. Its door was ajar. Dixon walked around Ethan.

Ethan's expression was dark and foreboding, but he followed Dixon into the room and shut the door behind him. "Okay, I'm here. What do we *need* to talk about?"

Dixon paced in front of the mirror that was actually two-way glass. He took a long breath, blew it out, then drew in another. He couldn't believe how hard his pulse was hammering. He'd known this wouldn't be easy, but he hadn't figured it would be this rough.

"Don't start again with all that stuff about my cousin." Ethan's voice carried a warning, but

Dixon heard something else in its tone, too. A growing apprehension. Did Ethan have an inkling of what Dixon was about to tell him?

He turned to face Ethan, who was still standing by the closed door, and placed his fists on his hips. "Did you get the name of the woman who lived in the house?"

"Renée Pettitpas?"

"No. She died a few months ago. I'm talking about the younger woman. The woman who was abducted."

Ethan nodded, although his expression didn't change. "Yes. Rose Bohème. Sounds like an alias to me."

Dixon wiped a hand down his face, then looked at Ethan. "It is an alias. For Rosemary Delancey. Your cousin is alive," he said.

"My—" Ethan stared at him. "My—" His face turned red and he doubled his fists. "Damn it, Dixon, you low-down—I'm not listening to this. I told you if you kept on—"

Dixon broke in. "Ethan, listen to me. I swear it's the truth."

Ethan's face drained of color. "If this is some kind of joke, I swear I'll kill you."

"No joke. No mistake." Dixon wiped a hand down his face. "I know how hard this is to believe. Trust me, I do. I didn't want to tell you until

I could—" he spread his hands "—could make sure she was safe, but—"

Ethan held up his hands. He still looked a little green around the gills. "Hold it. Just hold it!"

He pushed the fingers of both hands through his hair, tented his hands over his mouth and nose for a few breaths, then spread his palms. "I can't even take this in. I don't understand. I can't figure out—my cousin Rosemary—after twelve years—Why—how—"

"Delancey, sit down. You look like you're about to pass out."

Ethan scowled darkly. "I'll tell you what I'm about to do. I'm about to pound you into next week if you don't tell me just exactly what you're talking about. Because I don't believe she's alive. What I believe is that you have finally gone round the bend." His hands clenched into fists. "I told you to stop obsessing over her. I understand that she was your first case. I get that you want it closed. But damn it. It's been so long. It's not possible." He stopped and pushed his fingers through his hair again.

"Listen to me," Dixon pleaded. "She's got amnesia. The trauma of the attack was too much. She doesn't remember anything about the attack or anything before it."

"Amnes—" Ethan barked a short, unamused laugh. "Come on." He walked to the other side of the room, stood there with his back to Dixon for a few seconds, then whirled around. "You're telling me that this Bohème woman is my—" He stopped, as if he'd run out of steam.

"Son of a—" He rubbed his forehead, then his eyes. He looked up at Dixon, sucked in a deep breath, then started pacing. He tented his fingers over his mouth again. "Do you know what this is going to do to my family?"

"You can't tell them anything. Not yet."

Ethan whirled and glared at Dixon. "You think I'm stupid enough to go to them with this cock-and-bull story?" He laughed again, a dangerous sound. "You're completely crazy. My partner's lost his mind."

"Ethan, I can't force you to believe me, but I'm begging you to trust me. Rose is in danger, and I don't know where she is. The man who abducted her is the same man who tried to kill her back then."

Ethan just stared at him. "How in the hell do you know that?"

Dixon closed his eyes and turned away from Ethan, toward the mirror. "Because I'm the one who led him to her."

He felt Ethan's fist grab his sleeve and jerk him around. He didn't balk or duck, just went with the momentum and braced himself. He opened his eyes to a slit and saw Ethan pulling back his right fist, his teeth set in a grimace and his eyes dark as the night.

Dixon waited.

Ethan let go of his sleeve and cursed.

"Come on, Delancey. Hit me."

Ethan threw a derogatory name at him. "It's too easy. You're just standing there, hoping I'll knock all your teeth out because you know you deserve it." He did an about-face and walked over to the door. But instead of slamming it open and walking out, he leaned against the jamb.

Dixon watched him closely, but Ethan just looked back at him.

"What now?" Ethan finally asked. "What do we do now? How do we find her?"

Dixon breathed a sigh of relief. "That punk in the next room?" he said, gesturing. "I'll bet you a month's salary that he knows where she is, or at least who has her. I need to talk to him, see what he's willing to tell me." Dixon met Ethan's gaze. "I've LoJacked his car. I'm going to grill him enough that when he leaves here, I'm hoping he'll lead us to her."

"Let me get this straight," Ethan said, his voice and manner now deadly calm. "You found my cousin, you've been meeting with her, talking with her? You know she has amnesia? And now you're telling me you let some maniac abduct her? Oh and by the way, it's all your fault?"

Dixon's breath whooshed out in a frustrated sigh. "I can make it right. I can rescue her *if* I can get Junior to lead me to where she is."

"Fine," Ethan said on a sigh. "Fine. Are you going in to question him now?"

Dixon nodded.

"I've got to get some water," Ethan said. He still looked shell-shocked. "I'll be in the viewing room if you need me." He wrenched the door open and stalked out, not waiting for an answer from Dixon.

Dixon took a long, slow breath and rubbed his eyes. That went about as badly as he'd figured it would. Only he'd expected to be sporting a black eye or a sore jaw right about now. His partner had shown remarkable restraint.

He headed for the door of Interrogation Room One, but the computer tech stopped him.

"I've got the information from that phone." He handed Dixon the phone and a computer printout. "By the way, there's a message."

Dixon glanced at the phone's display. Sure enough it said *One new message*. He slipped it into his pocket and quickly scanned the printout. His eyes stopped on a familiar name and number.

Wexler. Where had he seen that name before? He pulled out his own phone and accessed the business directory Reed had sent him for the building on Tchoupitoulas. There it was, the first business on the list. *Aron Accounting.* Bruce Wexler was listed as the president and senior accountant. The car whose tag Thomas had memorized belonged to Aron Accounting, too.

Something Shively had said niggled at the edge of Dixon's brain. Something about the people who'd led the turf war that exploded when Innes had retired from the loan-sharking business. One of them had a name similar to the name of the accounting firm.

He snapped his fingers. That was it. Shively had said that an Aaron or Allen Wasabe was one of the contenders to take over the loan-sharking business when Innes retired.

Aron Accounting. Aron Wasabe.

Excitement rushed through Dixon's veins, energizing him. Was Aron Wasabe the monster who'd hurt Rose? And who had her in his clutches now?

He grabbed Junior's phone and accessed the message.

W needs u @ C.M. whs asap. call me.

Dixon opened the phone's inbox. There were other messages from Wexler. He strode over to the computer tech's desk.

"I need a transcript of all these messages," he said, holding out the phone.

"Done," the tech said, rooting around on his paper-littered desk. He picked up a sheet and handed it to Dixon.

"Why didn't you give this to me earlier?" Dixon

said, frowning as he skimmed the messages. They were incriminating, but none of them mentioned whs or C.M.

"You didn't ask for it."

Dixon wanted to grab the collar of the kid's shirt and jerk him up, but he restrained himself. "What do you think this means?" He held out the phone.

"C.M.? No clue. W-H-S is probably warehouse." The tech sent him a sidelong glance. "I'm assuming you know what the 'at' sign means."

Dixon ignored him. "What if I want to make sure I can track this phone, no matter whether it's on or off?"

The kid looked up at him, smirking. "Done."

"What do you mean, 'done'?"

"I mean I figured you might want to give it back to the guy. You know how there's a backup battery in cell phones?"

Dixon shrugged.

"Yeah, man. A lot of phones have a clock battery, so the time function is always running. So I took the GPS tracking off the main battery and hooked it to the backup. It won't last long, but it'll be on even if he turns the phone off."

"How long will it last?"

"Maybe twenty-four hours. Maybe less. Depends on how long he's had the phone—you know, how old the battery is."

"What the hell else did you do to it?"

"Nothing," he said, shaking his head. "It's a throwaway. Not much technology in there. Want to see the location?" He pointed at one of the computer screens where a red dot was blinking. "There you are, right in the middle of this building."

"What's the range of this thing?" Dixon said, tamping down on his excitement.

The kid shrugged. "I don't know, maybe twenty miles?"

"Is there any way I can see that from my car—like loaded into my car's GPS?"

"No, man." The kid laughed. "Not without some major equipment. But I can track it here and guide you."

"Good." Dixon pointed a finger at him. "You're officially on duty until I say otherwise."

"Sure, as long as I get overtime."

Dixon leaned over the desk and got in the kid's face. "Listen to me, punk. A woman's life is in danger. If I can't track this phone, she will *die*. Is that enough overtime for you?"

"Uh, yeah. I mean, yes, sir."

"Now, I want you to send a reply to Wexler's last message." It was a big risk, pretending to be Junior. Wexler could get suspicious and warn Wasabe. But Dixon figured it would be an even bigger risk to try to use Junior. The kid was already nearly paralyzed with fear.

"Type this. CM question mark. WHS question mark."

The tech did it, then handed the cell phone back to Dixon. He straightened and stalked toward Interrogation Room Two.

He'd known when he brought Junior here that he wouldn't get anything useful from him. He'd brought him solely to feed him a line. He needed Junior to believe that the police knew more than Dixon was letting on. He'd LoJacked Junior's car in hope that when he let him go, Junior would hightail it to the man who had taken Rose.

Now he had a better plan—he hoped.

A soft bell sounded from Junior's phone. A response from Wexler? Dixon checked the display. The message was cryptic.

Warehouse out Chef Menteur idiot. Ditch phone now.

Wexler was careful. Dixon would give Junior his cell phone back, and track him. Even if Junior tossed the cell phone, Dixon could track him with the LoJack.

If Junior drove directly to the warehouse. Dixon prayed that Wexler was summoning him to the same location where Rose was being held.

It was his only chance of saving her.

EVERY PART OF Rose's body hurt. She shifted, hoping to find a more comfortable position, but as soon as she straightened her leg, her calf knotted in a painful cramp. Instinctively she flexed her foot, but that just made her toes cramp.

Just don't move. Her entire being was focused on stopping the tearing pain. She tried to relax, even though her muscles felt as tight as springs.

Eventually, the pain let up, and as long as she remained perfectly still and relaxed, it stayed away.

Still and relaxed. She huffed. Piece of cake.

She focused on her surroundings—and her situation. Although that wasn't easy, either. Her head throbbed and when she tried to think, her brain felt as if it were wrapped in cotton. Everything was fuzzy.

Just as she'd experimented with tiny movements, she now exercised her hazy brain with small, careful thoughts. Like where was she? She carefully drew in a long breath. Someplace dark and musty, and smelling of something familiar. She couldn't identify it. The other smells were too strong.

How did she get here? Pushing through the haze in her brain, she tried to focus on the last thing she remembered.

The man—he'd forced his way into her house and shot her with something. Something that sent excruciating pain through her whole body until she'd apparently passed out. She didn't remember anything else until she'd woken up while he was dumping her into the trunk of a car. Then he'd shot her again.

The next thing she remembered was lying in a cramped fetal position in the dark, with rough woven fabric scratching her cheek. Even though her thinking was fuzzy, she'd recognized the uncomfortable compartment with the smell of oil and rubber in her nose and the feel of the road under her.

But now she'd been tossed onto a hard, rough, penetratingly cold surface. Her cheek burned and her hands and feet were numb.

She opened her eyes to a landscape of coarse, dirty concrete. Without moving her head, she sent her gaze around, taking in her surroundings. There was very little light coming in through several high, narrow windows of the warehouse. It seemed to be dark outside.

Warehouse. Of course. Now she saw the rivets in the metal walls. The giant wooden crates. The stacks of burlap sacks. She was in a coffee warehouse.

That explained the damp, musty odor, too. The warehouse was on the river.

Despair threatened to overtake her as all the separate bits of information her brain had been slowly processing slammed into her consciousness at once.

The pain. The car trunk. She'd been kidnapped and dumped in an abandoned warehouse! Terror burned through her from the top of her head to her toes, causing her muscles to cramp again.

Katrina had left dozens of abandoned warehouses around New Orleans in her wake. Maybe scores. She'd be as easy to find as a needle in a haystack.

Dixon had been right all along. Whoever had tried to kill her back then had found her again. She knew with a sickening certainty that Dixon had no idea where she was. The man had snatched her out of her own home and brought her here and nobody knew.

If she was going to survive, she'd have to save herself.

Where was he, by the way? Her kidnapper. Was he in the shadows watching her and laughing at her pain?

She opened her mouth and licked her lips. The tape he'd put over her mouth was gone. She took a huge breath. "Where are you, you coward!" she shouted, her neck and shoulder muscles tightening painfully with the effort.

She had to lay her head down on the floor until the muscle cramps subsided. She listened carefully, trying to hear a movement, a cough, anything that would tell her that the monster who'd kidnapped her was here.

She took a deep breath and tried again. "Are you hiding, watching me? Come out and show yourself like a man!" Her neck and shoulders seized again and she waited, panting, until they relaxed.

What was she doing? Certainly not accomplishing anything by yelling, except to exhaust herself.

Redoubling her determination, she took careful mental inventory of her body. Sometime while she was unconscious, her kidnapper had switched the elastic bandages on her wrists and ankles for cloth, which he'd wound around not just her wrists, but her forearms as well, and secured with duct tape. She couldn't see them, but she guessed her ankles and calves were bound the same way.

The way her arms were wrapped forced her elbows together in front of her and put a lot of pressure on her shoulders. Every slight movement made them feel as if they were being pulled out of their sockets.

In the dim light, she examined the duct tape that held the cloth in place. It was wrapped tightly, but without too much contortion, she should be able to grab an edge of the tape in her teeth. And if she could bite it, she could tear it—she hoped.

The first thing she had to do, before she could try to peel the duct tape off with her teeth, was sit up. She lay there for a few seconds, preparing for the agonizing task of rolling over and pushing herself upright. She took a long breath and started drawing up her legs.

If she couldn't get free of her bonds and somehow get out of here, the dark-eyed man who'd brought her here would kill her.

Chapter Fourteen

Dixon shook his head and glared at his partner. "No," he said firmly. "You *won't* be going with me. I need you on the GPS."

"I need to be there," Ethan had objected. "If you're right, that's my cousin."

"Listen to me, Delancey. I can take care of Rose. But I can't trust that smart-ass computer tech. If Junior leaves his car, I'm going to need you to guide me. It's the best chance we have."

Ethan looked at Dixon, then at his car. For a moment Dixon thought he was going to jump into the passenger seat and dare Dixon to drag him out bodily.

Finally, he huffed out a frustrated breath. "You're taking SWAT!" he commanded.

"I've got them on notice."

"On notice? No! You get them out there. They need to be in position."

"Ethan," Dixon said somberly, "if this is the same monster who attacked Rose, he cut her—cut her bad. If SWAT goes storming in, what's going to stop him from slitting her throat?"

Ethan winced and his face turned pale. "If you don't give them the location as soon as you have it, I will." He got in Dixon's face. "Do you understand me?"

"Sounds like a plan to me," Dixon said. "You give it to them—right after you tell me Junior's exact location."

"How do you know Junior won't just run?" Ethan asked.

"I looked him in the eye and told him I'd send him back to jail if he didn't tell me who had ordered him to watch Rose. He's too scared of this guy Wasabe to even blink at being threatened with prison."

Dixon studied Ethan.

"So can I count on you?" He held out his hand.

Ethan lifted his chin in a gesture that reminded Dixon of Rose, then after a second he shook Dixon's hand.

Dixon nodded and clapped his partner on the shoulder, then turned and got into his car. He called a number on his cell phone. "Okay," he said. "You can let Junior go now."

He'd had the receptionist hold off on giving Junior his belongings back until she heard from him. Now he waited for her to tell him that Junior had left the squad room.

"Okay, he just got on the elevator," she said.

"He's got his cell phone, right?"

"Right."

"Thanks, Ann," he said and hung up. Sure enough, within a couple of minutes, he saw Junior come tearing out of the front of the building, his cell phone to his ear. He headed straight for his car, which a uniformed policeman had brought to the station. Dixon started his engine and let it idle as he waited to see where Junior went.

He followed him east on Interstate 10. As he drove, he dialed Ethan and put his phone on Bluetooth, so he could hear Ethan through the radio speakers.

"So far he's heading out I-10," Ethan said. "Do you see him?"

"Yeah. I hope he's heading to that warehouse and I hope to God that's where Rose is. As long as he stays in his car, I've got him. If you'll stay there, I'll call you if the LoJack indicates that he's stopped."

"Okay. By the way, I'm keeping SWAT informed of your route," Ethan said. "They're coming up behind you."

"You make sure they hang back until *I* give the word."

"I heard you the first twenty times, Dix."

"At least he's heading toward Chef Menteur Highway."

"I guess," Ethan said. "There are dozens of abandoned warehouses out that way."

Dixon growled. "I know. And Rose is in one of them."

WASABE TURNED ONTO Chef Menteur Highway and hit the accelerator, climbing up to about ten miles per hour over the speed limit. It was after nine o'clock. He was late getting back to the warehouse. After Amy's soccer game was over, the Clampettes had cornered him and Carol, wanting to talk about getting together for dinner on the weekend.

He didn't know what The Boss was doing this evening that was going to make him late, but he sure hoped he was still doing it. Wasabe did not want The Boss to get to the warehouse before he did. He'd warned him not to go to his daughter's game, and he did not like to be disobeyed.

Damn he hated the man.

His car's Bluetooth buzzed. He glanced at the display on the dashboard. Speak of the devil. Grimacing, he pressed the answer button on the steering wheel. "Hello?"

"Where the hell are you?" The Boss's gravely voice demanded. "I'm here at the warehouse and I don't see your car."

"I'm almost there," Wasabe said as calmly and matter-of-factly as he could.

"Almost? Almost!" The Boss's voice reverberated through the car. "What did I tell you? How dare you disobey my specific orders!"

"Boss, I—"

But his effort at an explanation was drowned out by the cursing coming through his radio speakers. He clenched his fists around the steering wheel and determinedly kept his eyes on the road.

Once The Boss wound down, Wasabe spoke up. "I'm less than five minutes away," he said.

More cursing. "I'm ready to get this taken care of. Don't make me wait!"

Wasabe hung up the phone and wiped a hand down his face. He wasn't afraid of The Boss. Not physically. The man was about twenty years older than he was and not in good health, so he knew he could take him in a fight.

Plus, in this situation, The Boss needed him. The two of them were the only ones in the world who knew what had really happened on the night Rosemary Delancey disappeared, and why. The only other person who'd seen anything had died that night.

Wasabe turned off the highway and pulled around to the back side of the warehouse. He saw the black Lexus that belonged to The Boss. His headlights revealed that the only occupant of the car was the driver. A shiver of relief slid down his spine. Even though he wasn't really afraid of

The Boss, it was still good to know that the man was here alone.

He got out of the car and walked over to the driver's side window of The Boss's car, his right hand in his pocket, fingering the butterfly knife.

The Boss opened the door and got out. "You alone?"

"Yes, sir," Wasabe said. "How do you want to play this?"

The older man glared at him. "We've been over it. Don't tell me you've forgotten."

The Boss's voice and demeanor had taken on an uber-calmness that Wasabe recognized. When he contacted Wasabe to order a hit, it was always this voice he used. Different and much more terrifying than the fury he'd unleashed over the phone a few minutes before.

"Right," Wasabe said. "Just checking on the details. She's trussed just like you told me to do—nothing that will leave a mark. I've already got a tub full of river water. I'll hold her head under. Trussed up like she is, she won't be able to fight, so she should be dead in under two minutes."

The Boss nodded. "Where can I stand? I want to watch this. There will be no mistake this time."

"I can guarantee she'll be dead. I'll dump her body in the water and within twenty-four hours she'll be washed out to sea. You know I told you this area of the river has some killer whirlpools in it."

"Fine," the other man said. "Good. Let's get going."

Wasabe frowned. He wasn't sure exactly what The Boss's purpose was in wanting to watch Rosemary Delancey die. To tell the truth, he wasn't completely sure he understood what The Boss hoped to gain by killing her now, after all these years. Except revenge. And maybe that was it.

Maybe his whole purpose was to achieve closure. Wasabe shrugged to himself. Whatever The Boss wanted. All Wasabe was interested in was getting out from under the man's thumb.

"You're sure you want to be there?" he asked. Not many people were interested in actually witnessing the deaths they paid so dearly for. The Boss had never been—before.

"Don't ask me that again, punk," he said. "You botched everything last time. You know what you owe me, and I plan to stand right there and make sure not one thing goes wrong. Not this time."

There it was. The reason Wasabe was here. Every job he'd ever done, throughout his entire career, had been clean and clear. One-hundred percent satisfaction guaranteed and delivered. Except for this one. He'd been effectively indentured to The Boss for twelve years because of the two mistakes he'd made.

Now, finally, freedom was only a few minutes away. The Boss had promised him that as soon as Rosemary Delancey was dead and could never expose him, Wasabe could walk away.

He planned to retire and spend time with his wife and his little girl. He had enough money to be comfortable the rest of his life.

After he disposed of Rosemary Delancey, he only had one last job to do. He glanced at his watch. Junior Fulbright should be getting here soon.

He led The Boss to the unobtrusive door in the side of the warehouse. As he opened the door and gestured for The Boss to follow him into a small room that had once been an office, he spoke softly.

"The main floor is through that door. She's at the front near the roll-up doors. If you want, you can stand here in the doorway. Or if you want to be closer, you can hug the north wall and get as close as you want. There are no windows on that side. Either way, when I turn on the front row of lights, you'll still be in shadow. There's no way she can see you."

The Boss didn't say anything. He just nodded.

"Okay," Wasabe said. He could taste the freedom that was within his grasp. "Let's do this."

ROSE'S JAW ACHED and she felt like she was going to pull her front teeth right out of her gums. She'd been biting and pulling at the duct tape for what seemed like an hour. And in all that time she'd only managed to peel off a couple of narrow strips.

The first one had come off smoothly, unwinding three times from around her wrists. She'd had to stop, spit it out and grip another piece with her teeth.

But the second strip she'd managed to catch and pull had ripped away after only five inches or so.

She arched her neck and opened her mouth wide, stretching her jaw, trying to relax the aching muscles. She wriggled her cold, tingling fingers and bent her head to grab and peel another narrow strip. At the rate she was going, it could take all night to free her arms.

Then she heard something. She froze, holding her breath, but everything was quiet. What had she heard? A door? A river rat? The wind?

She bent her head and grabbed the frayed end of the duct tape between her teeth.

There it was again. That noise. Now she recognized it.

Terror ripped through her, paralyzing her. For a moment, all she could do was wait, unable to move, praying that she was wrong.

Let it be a rat, she begged, but she knew no four-legged vermin had made that noise. What she'd heard was footsteps on concrete. And as she held her breath, listening, they came closer, passed her and walked away.

Rose still didn't move a muscle. She waited, struggling to control her breathing, hoping that by some miracle the person walking toward her was not her abductor. But knowing with a grave certainty that he was.

Then suddenly, lights clicked on, blinding her. Her muscles, not entirely recovered from the taser, cramped and she whimpered involuntarily.

"Hi, Rosemary," the voice from her nightmares said.

She couldn't see, couldn't open her eyes even to a squint, because of the brightness of the lights. She heard the footsteps approaching, closer and closer.

She cringed.

"Well, look at you, little Irish Rose," the man said, his voice grating along her nerve endings.

Rissshhhh, rozzzzzsss. Rissshhhh, rozzzzzsss.

"Look at you. You figured out that you could get yourself untied," he said, sounding genuinely impressed. "If you had eight or ten hours. You know, I thought from the beginning that you were a remarkably brave young woman."

Rose managed to open her eyes to narrow slits and look at him. She still thought the face was vaguely familiar, but she didn't remember it. Not really. She did, however, know that voice. It still haunted her dreams.

"I apologize for what I did to you, Rosemary. Given my preference, I would have made it quick and clean, like I plan to do now." As he spoke, he pulled something from his pocket and held it up. It was silver—made of some kind of metal.

Rose's pulse thrummed painfully in her throat and a chill slid down her spine.

As he flipped his wrist, a silvery flash blinded her.

She screamed.

"So you do remember," he said, flipping his wrist again. Another flash, this time accompanied by the *snick-snick* of metal on metal.

As tears welled in her eyes and rolled down her cheeks, the man stepped around behind her and grabbed a fistful of her hair. He pulled her head back.

Rose bit her lips nearly through, tasting blood. She was not going to scream or whimper again. She was not going to give the monster the satisfaction of hearing her beg.

Dixon's navy blue eyes and beautiful smile rose before her inner vision. She loved him so much. Partly because he'd tried so hard to save her, and partly because for twelve years he'd never given up on finding her. Mostly, though, she loved him because of the kind of man he was.

Dixon, I'm sorry. I wanted to live my life with you. Dear God, please let him know that.

The man jerked her hair hard enough to bring more tears to her eyes. Then he lay the blade of the knife against the left side of her throat, under her ear. She felt the sting as the sharp blade sank into her skin.

"Do you know how bad I want to shoot you right now, Junior?" Dixon growled. He had the punk spread-eagled across the hood of his car. "There's a woman in there—" he indicated the dilapidated warehouse "—who might be dead—" His voice broke on the word. He cleared his throat.

"Who might be dead right now, and it's your fault. I swear you'll go to prison for this and your skinny butt probably won't last a week."

"Don't—please—" Junior blubbered. His whole body was quaking. "I didn't—I didn't know what he was doing. I swear he didn't tell me anything. Please!" He started crying like a baby.

Dixon dragged the punk over to his car and threw him to the ground. He cuffed him around the car's axle with his arms stretched as far as they would go. There was no way Junior could escape. Hell, he could barely move. Dixon stuffed his handkerchief in Junior's mouth and left him there.

He glanced around, wondering how far away

the SWAT team was. It hardly mattered, though, because Dixon wasn't about to wait for them. What he'd told Junior was true. Rose could be dead by now. Dixon had to get in there. If she was still alive, he didn't want to waste one second.

For the first time, he turned his attention to the cars that were parked in the shade of the warehouse. One was the sedan owned by Aron Accounting. The other was a black Lexus. He didn't know whose it was and he didn't care. The SWAT team and the local police could figure that out.

All Dixon wanted to do was find Rose. He saw the small door in the side of the building, a darker rectangle than the metal walls. It was slightly ajar. So he stepped over to it, drawing his weapon, and slipped inside.

It took his eyes a few long seconds to dark-adapt. Finally he was able to distinguish walls and furniture. It was a small room, maybe an office, judging by the silhouettes of file cabinets and desks. At the far end of the room was another door standing ajar. Pale light glowed from the room beyond. He heard voices echoing as if they were bouncing off the metal walls of an empty room. The main room of the warehouse.

Dixon moved silently over to the lit doorway. He flattened himself against the wall, his weapon at the ready, and listened.

"Stop!" a commanding voice said.

Dixon froze. Had he been spotted? But the voice kept talking.

"What the hell are you doing? Get that knife away from her throat."

At the same time, he heard a soft, feminine whimper.

A relief so profound it brought tears to his eyes whooshed through Dixon. Rose was alive. For now. The muscles in his arms and legs quivered like jelly. He took a deep silent breath and tightened his grip on his handgun. Had someone else come to Rose's rescue?

"I just wanted to scare her, Boss," a second voice responded.

"Get those bindings off her arms and legs," the commanding voice continued. "Now!"

While the voice was speaking, Dixon had eased the door open several inches, enough that he could slip through. His initial urge was to rush forward and join the man who sounded like he was rescuing Rose. But something held him back—maybe the fact that the man with the knife had called the other man Boss.

The sight that greeted Dixon took his breath away. Rose was on her knees, her legs and forearms bound with some kind of cloth. Standing behind her was a wiry man with his fist in her hair and what looked like a butterfly knife held to her throat.

As Dixon watched, the man shrugged, then with lightning-fast precision, he slit the cloth bindings on her arms.

Rose cried out as the cloths fell away. When the man let go of her hair, she collapsed like a rag doll.

"Her feet, Wasabe," The Boss said.

So that was Wasabe. Dixon watched as he slit the bindings on her feet and legs.

Dixon moved carefully and quietly out of the doorway. He stood, his feet apart, and aimed the barrel of the gun at Wasabe's head, holding it with both hands for steadiness and accuracy. He didn't want to make himself known as long as Wasabe still held the knife.

He would wait for The Boss to make his move, then back him up.

"Put the knife away and get on with it," The Boss said and stepped out of the shadows.

When the pale light played over The Boss's features, Dixon gaped. He *knew* him. Immediately, he understood why he was determined to stop Wasabe from hurting Rose.

At that instant The Boss raised his arms and leveled the barrel of a gun at the man's head. Dixon rose to the balls of his feet, ready to help him stop Wasabe from killing Rose.

Chapter Fifteen

Rose couldn't believe her ears. She knew that voice, didn't she?

"Lyndon?" she said, not completely sure where the name or the memory of the voice came from. All she knew was that they were emerging from behind the blank wall in her brain that blocked her past from her.

But hadn't Dixon told her that Lyndon was dead? That he'd been killed by the same man who'd tortured her? This man who'd brought her here.

Wasabe laughed as he dragged a galvanized tub over near her. Then he grabbed her hair again. "Not Lyndon, little Irish Rose," he said, dragging her toward the tub.

"Wait, Wasabe," Lyndon's voice said.

Wasabe clenched his fist more tightly in her hair, bringing tears to her eyes again. "What is it now, Boss? Want to tell her why you're doing this?

Get on with it, then, because I'm tired. I'd like to get this over with and get home."

"Are you threatening me?"

No, Rose realized. That voice wasn't Lyndon's. It was older, deeper and the tone was ominous. The voice she remembered had never sounded like that.

"No, Boss," Wasabe's tone turned from impatient to placating. "It's just that I've waited for twelve years for this, just like you have. I'm as ready to be done with it as you are."

"You're right," the voice said. "I am ready to be done with it. I'm tired of listening to your rusty voice and your excuses. This is for killing my son."

"Wha—" Wasabe started, but his voice was drowned out by a loud pop.

Rose jumped. Wasabe's hand released her hair. She threw herself to the side, away from him, but he didn't come after her.

He dropped to the concrete floor like a rock.

Rose whirled. Dark blood covered the front of his shirt, and his eyes were open and staring. She covered her mouth with her hands and turned her gaze to the man who had shot him.

It was Eldridge Banker, Lyndon's father.

"M-Mr. Banker—" she stammered as he came toward her and grabbed her arm, pulling her to her feet. He dragged her up close to him, his dark eyes staring into hers.

"I tried to save you," he said, "but I was too late."

Rose stared at him, trying to make sense out of what he was saying. "No," she said. "It's okay. I'm okay."

But Lyndon's father shook his head. "No. I'm so sorry. I really tried."

He must be talking about before. "I'm sorry, too," Rose said. "I'm so sorry Lyndon was killed." She moved to step away from him, but he tightened his grip.

"At least you managed to get Wasabe's gun away from him and shoot him," Banker went on in that somber, deadly tone. "But seeing Wasabe triggered your lost memories of that night, and you realized Lyndon, the man you loved, was dead."

"Gun?" Rose echoed.

"Devastated now that you remembered your fiancé, you wrote a note, explaining that you and Lyndon were secretly married before he died. Then you turned Wasabe's gun on yourself and committed suicide."

Rose shook her head. "No, no, that's not right. What are you talking about?"

"I've got your marriage license right here," Banker said. "Lyndon had put it in his safety deposit box."

"Mr. Banker, I don't understand," Rose said. But she was afraid she was beginning to. Had Lyndon's father been looking for her all this time to kill her?

"Don't you?" he asked. "It's simple. Surely, you knew Lyndon well enough to know what a good-for-nothing he was. His gambling bankrupted me." He gestured toward the dead man with a nod. "Wasabe was supposed to scare you into giving him your money. Clever of your grandfather to put it in trust until you were twenty-five."

Rose's head was spinning. Banker's words were triggering fragments of memories. "He kept telling me to give him the money and he'd stop," she said, turning her head toward the man Banker had shot. "But I couldn't. I didn't have any money to give him."

"Well, you do now," Banker said. "Now shut up and listen. I've got two documents for you to sign. Your suicide note and your marriage license. Your note is simple and to the point. Now that you remember your fiancé—no, your husband—you can't live without him."

"You're crazy!" She yanked against his punishing fingers. "You had your own son murdered?"

Banker jerked her up against him. "He wasn't supposed to die!" he spat. "And neither were you. I waited twelve years for Wasabe to find you. Why do you think I shot him? He murdered my son."

Banker forced Rose over to a table and shoved her down in a chair. "Don't move or I'll shoot you in the leg."

"No, you won't. Not if you want the police to believe I killed myself."

Banker's already red face turned purple. "Shut up! I don't need you. I'll forge your handwriting. Nobody will question it after all this time." Suddenly, he raised his arm and swung the butt of the gun at her head.

Rose dived, turning over the wooden chair. Banker's gun scraped the side of her head as she fell. She scrambled away, trying to get her feet under her so she could run. But her feet were still numb from being tied up. She tripped and fell.

At the very instant she hit the floor a shot rang out.

Rose stiffened, waiting for the unimaginable pain of a bullet tearing into her flesh, but it didn't come.

Behind her, Eldridge Banker grunted. Rose heard the clatter of heavy metal against the concrete floor, then the thunk of a body.

She twisted around. Banker was down, the gun he'd held lying about a foot from his hand. Crying, panting, Rose flung herself toward the weapon, reaching for it.

"Rose!"

She heard the voice, but she didn't believe her

ears or her brain. She was too confused, too stunned
by what had happened to trust anything. She had
to get to the gun. She was in an abandoned warehouse with two men who wanted her dead. It didn't
matter that they were both on the floor with blood
spilling onto the concrete. They'd tried to kill her
and Banker's gun was the closest weapon.

She reached out and wrapped her fingers around
the barrel of the gun, eyeing Banker, terrified that
he'd grab her again.

"Rose, stop! That gun's loaded!"

She gripped the handle of the gun and pointed
it toward the familiar, treacherous voice. Lyndon's
voice hadn't been Lyndon. There was no way that
the voice she was hearing now was really Dixon.

Pointing the gun toward the voice, she shouted,
"Don't come near me! I'll shoot!"

"Rose, it's me. It's Dixon. SWAT is right behind me."

She shook her head. "No, you can't be Dixon.
He's not here. Who are you?" She had her back
to Banker and Wasabe, and she didn't like that,
so she scooted sideways, so she could see each
of them and keep the gun trained on the bodiless
voice coming from the shadows.

"I'm coming closer, Rose. Be careful. It's me,
Dixon. Remember? You told my fortune?"

It was Dixon. She shook her head. No. It couldn't
be.

As she watched, holding the gun in both hands

and aiming in the direction of the voice, she saw a movement in the shadows. She sat up straighter and held the gun out at arm's length.

It was heavy.

"Rose, it's me," he said, moving closer. "I was afraid I'd never find you."

He kept saying things—repeating things he'd said to her. Her arms were trembling, still shaky and weak from being bound. And the gun was so heavy.

He stepped out of the shadows, his broad shoulders and blue-black hair so familiar. He had his hands up, palms out. She saw the silhouette of a gun in his waistband.

He took one more step and the light caught his eyes—his navy blue eyes. They were glistening oddly.

"I'm so sorry, Rose. I swore I'd keep you safe and I didn't." He took a shuddering breath. "I was afraid the way Banker was holding on to you I wouldn't be able to get a shot off before he killed you—" His voice broke.

Rose stared at him. He was there. Strong, confident and everything she'd never known she wanted.

"Dixon—" she said and let the gun fall from her fingers as she tried to stand.

He ran to her and lifted her into his arms.

She buried her face in the curve of his neck and

cried as doors crashed open and the SWAT team stormed the warehouse.

THE NEXT AFTERNOON Rose stood in Maman's living room, letting her fingertips drift over the ivory keys of Maman's grand piano. She didn't try to play. She wouldn't have been able to distinguish the keys through her tear-filled eyes.

The night before had been as chaotic and confusing as a Mardi Gras parade. Just as Dixon was promising to stay at her side, no matter what, someone had whisked her away and deposited her in front of a female emergency medical technician, who gave her a quick examination and pronounced her unhurt. She gave Rose two tablets in a small envelope and told her to take them if she had trouble sleeping.

Then a police detective had cornered her and fired questions at her about what had happened, from the moment she'd first seen Aron Wasabe.

A young man in jeans and an NOPD jacket took her fingerprints, swabbed her fingers and palms with a giant cotton swab that he stored in a plastic tube, then swabbed the inside of her cheek with another swab. "Just routine," he'd told her with an engaging smile.

In the middle of all that, she'd watched EMTs crowding around Eldridge Banker, then placing him on a gurney and rushing him out of the warehouse. Aron Wasabe's body was carried out, too, in a body bag.

By the time Dixon had made it back to her side, she'd been numb with cold and exhaustion. So he'd brought her home, watched to make sure she took the tablets the EMT had given her, and put her to bed, promising to stay with her all night.

When she'd finally woken up around noon, she'd found a note on her bedside table.

Gone to work. I'll be back as soon as I can. REST! Love, D.

Rose stopped playing with the piano keys and picked up her mug of tea. It was cold, so she went into the kitchen to warm it in the microwave. As she took a careful sip to test its heat, she heard the doorbell ring. Then she heard the lock click open.

"Rose?"

It was Dixon. A flurry of emotions kicked her pulse into high gear. Paramount was the fear of facing him in the light of day. He'd said things to her last night, things she wanted to believe so badly her heart ached. But did she dare?

"Rose, can we come up? I've got someone with me."

"Sure—" she tried to call, but her voice was raspy. She cleared her throat. "Sure." She looked down at herself. She had on the kimono over her nightgown and one of Maman's lacy shawls over that. Decent enough for giving a statement to the police, she supposed.

She listened to the hard, masculine footsteps on the stairs as she put on more water to heat for tea. When she turned around, Dixon was standing in the kitchen doorway with a younger man standing beside him.

"How're you doing this morning?" Dixon asked. "Did you sleep late?"

She nodded with a forced smile. "I didn't wake up until around noon. Would you—either of you—like some tea?"

"I had coffee," Dixon said as he turned to look at the second man. "Rose—this is my partner. Ethan Delancey."

The name cut through her like a knife. She stared at him—she couldn't tear her eyes away. His hair was dark and his eyes were an odd golden-brown. He smiled tentatively and nodded a cautious greeting.

"Ethan is your cousin," Dixon said gently.

"E-Ethan," she said, trying out the name. "I—I don't know what to say." She caught the edges of the shawl and wrapped it tightly around her.

"It's okay," Ethan said, holding his hands out, palms up. "I don't either—except that I'm so glad to see you. So glad you're not—"

"Dead?" she finished for him on a laugh. "Me, too. But it's not quite that simple."

Ethan nodded. "Dixon filled me in, finally. You don't remember anything from before your attack?"

Rose compressed her lips and shook her head. "Last night, during all that happened, I began to remember things. Mostly about the attack. It was strange." She stopped, trying to think how to describe the sensations. "Kind of like a double exposure. You know? Like two movies running at the same time on the same screen." She stopped talking and looked at Ethan more closely.

"You're my cousin? How, exactly?"

Ethan sent Dixon a quick glance. "I tell you what, Rosemary. You're trying to process a lot of stuff right now. Why don't I come back this evening and we can talk some more. Your—" He paused for a second, then continued. "A member of our family is a chef. I'll pick up something for dinner."

Rose nodded. "Okay," she said, her lips feeling numb.

"You, too, Dix," Ethan said. "Bring the wine."

Dixon looked at Rose. "If it's okay with you," he said.

She lifted her shoulders.

"Okay, then," Ethan broke in. "I've got to be going. I'll see you two tonight." And he turned and left.

Rose stared after him. Her cousin. She rubbed

the scar at her hairline. She was a Delancey, and she had a cousin. In fact, based on the website she'd seen, she had brothers, cousins, aunts and uncles—and parents. A slew of people she was about to meet for the first time.

The safe life Maman had so carefully structured for her was nothing but a memory now.

"Rose?" Dixon's voice broke into her thoughts.

She lifted her chin and met his gaze. "Why did you bring him here?"

Dixon's gaze faltered. "He's my partner, and your cousin. He wanted to see you."

Rose shook her head. "I know all that, but that's not why you did it."

"The police commissioner is keeping your identity secret for now, but it won't last long. It will be leaked and then you're going to be bombarded by the press. You need to be prepared."

"How long?" she asked, panic fluttering like butterfly wings under her breastbone.

"Probably within twelve hours, if we're lucky. A lot sooner, if we're not."

"Oh," she said, feeling like she'd been punched in the stomach. "What—what should I do?"

Dixon was watching her carefully, an odd, cautious expression on his face. "Why don't you come stay with me for a few days, until you're ready to go home to your parents and brothers? If you stay here, you won't be able to set foot outside without someone taking your picture or asking questions. If you come home with me, I can protect you."

Rose's eyes pricked with tears. It was what he'd told her from the first moment she'd met him. He could protect her, and he had.

"What about you?" she asked. "Isn't your case closed now?"

He nodded. "I just got word this morning that the second sample of blood on your robe is a match for Aron Wasabe. So, yeah, it's closed." He looked down at his hands. "I don't have that excuse anymore."

"Excuse?" she echoed.

"For my entire career, people have made fun of me for being so obsessed with my first case. The Beauty Queen Murder. So my excuse was that it was the only case I'd never managed to close. But that's not why I was obsessed."

"No?" she said breathlessly.

He shook his head. "No. I was obsessed with you." He looked up and his navy blue eyes were wet with tears. "I told you, I was afraid I'd never find you. I was afraid I was doomed to spend my life in love with a dead woman."

Rose was stunned. She'd always hoped Maman's romantic prophecies would come true, but she'd never dared believe it.

"That night," she said, "when I woke up with Maman wrapping bandages around my hands and arms, she told me that she would keep me safe until my dark angel brought my memories and my grief back to me."

Dixon's brows drew down into a frown.

"That was only one of the predictions she had for me, and as obscure as they were, I see now that they've all come true."

Dixon looked so bewildered that Rose chuckled and with her fingertip, smoothed the wrinkle between his brows. "She told me my destiny lay in the hands of the Fool. And when she was no longer here, I should watch for my dark angel. That he would protect me."

She touched Dixon's hand. "Maman knew you would come," she said, her own eyes filling with tears.

Dixon blinked furiously against the stinging in his eyes as he shook his head. "You've been through a lot, Rose. Too much for anyone to bear. You need time. Time to get to know your family. Time to get past what just happened."

He took a deep breath. "You're going to have to testify at Eldridge Banker's trial. I shot him in the stomach and it looks like he's going to survive. You don't need any more stress right now."

"Dixon—" she said, her face looking stricken.

He knew she'd come to depend on him during the past few horror-filled days. But once she'd had time to relearn who she was and to live without doubt and fear, she'd realize she no longer needed him.

"I am so glad I found you," he said. "I am so glad you're okay and that you can go back to your family. They love you—"

"Oh no, you don't," she snapped, pushing her index finger into his chest. "You are *not* walking out on me."

"No, of course not," he said quickly. "I meant it when I said you could stay with me. I've got a guest room with its own bath. The sink drips, but I've been meaning to fix it." He looked at her, then at the floor. "No. What you ought to do is stay with your parents. That's probably better. They have resources—"

"You listen to me, Dixon Lloyd. From the first moment I met you, you've been trying to run my life. You've been bullying me, making me do what *you* thought was best. Well, it's time for a change."

Dixon opened his mouth to speak, but Rose held up her hand with a don't-mess-with-me expression. "Maman told me something else. She said my dark angel would try to sacrifice himself for me. She said not to let him. She told me that the Chinese believe if you save someone's life you're responsible for them." She poked him in the chest again.

"That means *you* are responsible for *me*. So what are you going to do about me?"

Dixon was speechless. "I…" He literally couldn't speak. His throat was too tight.

Rose gave a frustrated sigh and stepped up to him, lifted her head and kissed him.

Dixon couldn't resist. He'd lived through years of hell, afraid that he was searching in vain for a ghost. He'd spent hours of hell the day before, afraid that Wasabe had killed her. Now her very alive, very sensual mouth was on his and he couldn't do a thing except take her in his arms and kiss her back.

After a long time, he whispered against her lips. "I love you, Rose, more than you can ever know."

"Don't you ever stop," she whispered back.

After another few moments, Dixon pulled back and looked into Rose's amber eyes. "I think I've figured out what I need to do," he said softly, smiling at her.

"Oh yeah?" she responded. "This better be good."

"Since I'm responsible for you, it's going to be important to keep you close. The only way I can think of to do that is to marry you."

Rose regarded him somberly for so long that his heart squeezed painfully. Was she going to turn him down?

Finally she spoke. "The only way, eh?" she said. "Okay, then. I guess that'll do," she replied. "Don't get the idea you can bully me, though."

"Never," he laughed and held out his arms. "Now come here," he said.

Rose stepped into the arms of the man who had loved her for longer than she could remember.

* * * * *

LARGER-PRINT BOOKS!

GET 2 FREE LARGER-PRINT NOVELS PLUS
2 FREE GIFTS!

❧ Harlequin®

INTRIGUE®

BREATHTAKING ROMANTIC SUSPENSE

YES! Please send me 2 FREE LARGER-PRINT Harlequin Intrigue® novels and my 2 FREE gifts (gifts are worth about $10). After receiving them, if I don't wish to receive any more books, I can return the shipping statement marked "cancel." If I don't cancel, I will receive 6 brand-new novels every month and be billed just $5.24 per book in the U.S. or $5.99 per book in Canada. That's a saving of at least 13% off the cover price! It's quite a bargain! Shipping and handling is just 50¢ per book in the U.S. and 75¢ per book in Canada.* I understand that accepting the 2 free books and gifts places me under no obligation to buy anything. I can always return a shipment and cancel at any time. Even if I never buy another book, the two free books and gifts are mine to keep forever.

199/399 HDN FERE

Name _____ (PLEASE PRINT) _____

Address _____ Apt. # _____

City _____ State/Prov. _____ Zip/Postal Code _____

Signature (if under 18, a parent or guardian must sign)

Mail to the **Reader Service:**
IN U.S.A.: P.O. Box 1867, Buffalo, NY 14240-1867
IN CANADA: P.O. Box 609, Fort Erie, Ontario L2A 5X3
Not valid for current subscribers to Harlequin Intrigue Larger-Print books.

**Are you a subscriber to Harlequin Intrigue books
and want to receive the larger-print edition?
Call 1-800-873-8635 today or visit www.ReaderService.com.**

* Terms and prices subject to change without notice. Prices do not include applicable taxes. Sales tax applicable in N.Y. Canadian residents will be charged applicable taxes. Offer not valid in Quebec. This offer is limited to one order per household. All orders subject to credit approval. Credit or debit balances in a customer's account(s) may be offset by any other outstanding balance owed by or to the customer. Please allow 4 to 6 weeks for delivery. Offer available while quantities last.

Your Privacy—The Reader Service is committed to protecting your privacy. Our Privacy Policy is available online at www.ReaderService.com or upon request from the Reader Service.

We make a portion of our mailing list available to reputable third parties that offer products we believe may interest you. If you prefer that we not exchange your name with third parties, or if you wish to clarify or modify your communication preferences, please visit us at www.ReaderService.com/consumerschoice or write to us at Reader Service Preference Service, P.O. Box 9062, Buffalo, NY 14269. Include your complete name and address.

HILP11B

The series you love are now available in

LARGER PRINT!

The books are complete and unabridged—
printed in a larger type size to make it
easier on your eyes.

Harlequin®
Romance

From the Heart, For the Heart

Harlequin®
INTRIGUE®
BREATHTAKING ROMANTIC SUSPENSE

Harlequin®
Presents®

Seduction and Passion Guaranteed!

Harlequin®
Super Romance®

Exciting, emotional, unexpected!

Try **LARGER PRINT** today!

Visit: www.ReaderService.com
Call: 1-800-873-8635

Harlequin®

A *Romance* FOR EVERY MOOD™

www.ReaderService.com

HLPDIR11